BY

JULIA PHILLIPS

Disappearing Earth

Bear

BEAR

BEAR

A NOVEL

JULIA PHILLIPS

HOGARTH

NEW YORK

Copyright © 2024 by Julia Phillips
Map copyright © 2024 by David Lindroth Inc.

Published in the United States by Hogarth,
an imprint of Random House, a division of
Penguin Random House LLC, New York.

HOGARTH is a trademark of the
Random House Group Limited, and the H colophon
is a trademark of Penguin Random House LLC.

Hardback ISBN: 9780525520436
Ebook ISBN: 9780525520443

Printed in the United States of America on acid-free paper

randomhousebooks.com

2 4 6 8 9 7 5 3 1

FIRST EDITION

Book design by Barbara M. Bachman

For Alex and
our two beloved cubs

"Poor bear," said the mother, "lie down by the fire, only take care that you do not burn your coat." Then she cried: "Snow-white, Rose-red, come out, the bear will do you no harm, he means well." So they both came out, and by-and-by the lamb and dove came nearer, and were not afraid of him. The bear said: "Here, children, knock the snow out of my coat a little"; so they brought the broom and swept the bear's hide clean; and he stretched himself by the fire and growled contentedly and comfortably. It was not long before they grew quite at home, and played tricks with their clumsy guest. They tugged his hair with their hands, put their feet upon his back and rolled him about, or they took a hazel-switch and beat him, and when he growled they laughed.

—BROTHERS GRIMM

SAN JUAN ISLANDS

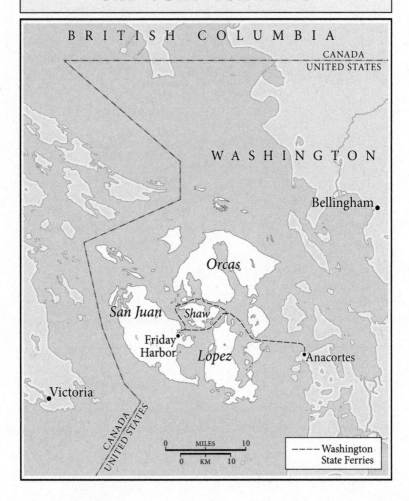

BEAR

THE FERRY FROM FRIDAY HARBOR LEFT FOURTEEN TIMES a day—fifteen on weekends—to loop around San Juan Channel's scattered islands. Every trip lasted at least sixty-five minutes. Too long. Sam spent that whole time, hours daily, tourist season after tourist season, in the galley making coffee for people who treated her like a peasant.

Like Cinderella picking lentils from the ashes, Sam was a nobody doing work that meant nothing, but no prince was ever going to pluck her out of this. She saw them all the time on the boat, those royal types: the usual wealthy with their salt-and-pepper hair and orthodontist-straightened smiles. The celebrities and Seattle tech millionaires, meanwhile, glowed at the gas station after getting to the island by private plane. They didn't see her. They never would. Young as she was, Sam had lived long enough to know who could be counted on and who couldn't, who could be trusted and who had to be put up with in order to pay the bills. Broad-shouldered men lined up before her all day long; it didn't matter. Elena was the only one who would save her from this place. They were going to have to save each other.

Sam's station was a little box trapped inside a big one, a high-walled beverage and snack counter at the center of a wide room lined by fluorescent lights and shatterproof windows. Outside those windows, the waves rippled, the clouds shifted. Sometimes a dock appeared. Passengers shuffled on and off. The dock receded. Under the lights, people yelled after their misbehaving children. They made ostentatious plans for how they would spend their vacations: kayaking? Beachcombing? Visiting the lavender farms? They stared through Sam to the food display cases and asked whether the boat's prepackaged cinnamon rolls were any good. She said they were. They weren't. Whether she recommended the pastries or suggested a pretzel or warned them about eating chowder on rough seas, the tourists barely touched the counter's tip jar, which was wrapped with a paper sign exhorting them to be kind and consider generosity.

Some tiny part of her couldn't blame them. After this long in food service, Sam, too, had stopped considering generosity. Now it was all bare routine. Brew the coffee. Dump the grounds. Restock the sugar packets. Get through one more shift.

Sam made twenty-four dollars an hour riding across gray waters, selling plastic-sheathed cookies and bags of chips. Ten dollars above minimum wage—one dollar for every year of her life spent at the whim of the Washington

State Department of Transportation. Good money, if she actually got reliable shifts, but she'd never yet been able to stitch together a living.

A decade earlier, high school diploma in hand, Sam had pictured making a salary they could count on. Even flourish with. Elena had paid for Sam to get a merchant mariner certification so Sam could work for the ferries—those were good jobs, state jobs, with benefits and a pension and health insurance that would cover the whole family. But the state didn't hire Sam. They didn't even interview her. Nothing she had counted on back then had come to pass. Elena'd had to scramble to get Sam a job with her at the golf club, where management didn't like Sam and Sam didn't like them, and the club members told long, dull stories about their days on the green, and everyone complained about how their drinks were mixed. When, finally, dining opened on the ferries, it seemed a small miracle: Sam was certified, qualified, experienced. Elena was relieved. The ferry's dining vendor did hire Sam. They paid her. They got her into a routine, and then the pandemic arrived, and sailings were canceled, and the galleys shut down, and they dropped her for two years.

Two years at home. Two years with nothing better. The club wouldn't hire Sam back at that point; they said they could barely afford to keep Elena on as it was. Fewer tourists were coming. On the island, Sam only saw boutique coffee shops with narrowing hours, second homes that needed less cleaning, fancy restaurants that would never

employ her anyway because she had bad people skills and
fucked-up teeth. After Sam ran through her unemploy-
ment, she started taking online surveys for cash, but those
didn't deliver the big bucks, either—a couple dollars for
every hour tallied, maybe. She drove their mother to doctors' appointments, sat in parking lots to tap through mar-
ket research questions on her phone, and took the meager
payments that arrived.

Their family had had to put so much on Elena's credit
cards these past couple years. Sixty-five hundred dollars,
which had turned, with interest, into nearly eleven thousand, the last Sam heard. And then their car broke down
over the winter. The cost of their mother's medication
went up. When, in April, the state announced they were
reopening ferry dining, Elena put her head down on their
kitchen table, and Sam said, "Are you crying?"

Elena looked up, dry-eyed. Worn out. "No," she said.
Then: "But thank God."

Sam didn't see any reason for gratitude. She'd been back
in the galley more than a month now, and things were as
tight as they'd always been. She was still taking her phone
surveys, though sometimes she'd forfeit even those if the
boat left an island and she lost cell service before she finished filling one out. Tourists interrupted her with inane
questions about the Lummi Nation as if Sam had the time
to go to canoe landing ceremonies or make herself an expert on San Juan's history. Elena, meanwhile, was trying to
keep her tips, stinking of hamburger grease from the club's

grill, on top of the refrigerator as an emergency fund, but emergencies kept coming, kept taking. Everything they made was siphoned away by taxes and bills and their mother's healthcare costs.

How exhausting. This slog. Endless. No matter their jobs or their wages, this is how things would be, as long as they lived on the island. They would have to move, Sam always told Elena, if they wanted a life worth living. And Elena didn't disagree. They didn't even have to discuss it: the necessity of moving. Both had committed long ago.

These days, Elena only quibbled over the details. That was her role, maybe, as the older sister, to think more practically. They would need savings to go, Elena said, and they didn't have any; they had to pay this, and that, and here, and there, and . . .

Friday Harbor was behind Sam now. Ahead of her. Behind. Across the waves, along the channel, as the ferry orbited the center of Sam's tiny universe. Black seabirds swooped along the water. The islands of the archipelago made an unending series of green velvet mounds. Over their shorelines, shining white buildings sat on stacked hills. Years ago, before Elena devoted her time to fretting over a million logistics, she had told Sam that they did have one way out of this place: the house. Sell the house, and their better future would at last arrive.

The house was a 1979 vinyl-sided nightmare, a too-small two-bedroom bought by their grandmother with her survivors benefits after their grandfather passed. She must have imagined, then, that it would be a stepping-stone to lift their family through the middle class. It wasn't. It hung heavy around their necks. Their grandmother had died in that house, and their mother brought Elena and Sam into the world there. Around them all, the place had aged. The trim under its stair treads bent off. The wall paint, peach and pastel, was peeling. The tiles in the shower were cracked, letting water seep into the house's body, where it sat and rotted, degrading what little legacy their grandmother had left.

But awful as it was, it was still a property on scenic San Juan Island. The house sat on six wooded acres five miles outside town. That land was gold. Useless as it weighed on their family for now, it would mean something to somebody, someday.

The sisters had shared a bedroom until the summer before Sam's senior year, when Elena, newly graduated, moved to the living room. Elena at eighteen was restless, wilder. More willing to chatter with Sam about the possibility of their dreams. One night, after Sam crept out to spend time together before sleep, they sat on the sofa, pillow and blanket balled alongside, and Elena set out the whole plan.

Their mother had already started, at that point, to cut back her schedule at the salon. Her breath was short. She felt chest pressure. Elena saw how tired she was, how much weaker she was growing, and understood—she needed them. So they would stay, Elena told Sam. They would take care of their mother, as she'd taken care of their grandmother, until she didn't need care anymore. Eventually they would inherit, then sell, the house, and use the proceeds to set themselves up elsewhere. A place where they could do what they wanted. Slog less, live more. Become the people they had never before had the freedom to be.

That night, Elena guessed they might only have a couple years left with their mother. Five, at most. They had to spend that precious time with her.

It rocked Sam, a wake against her body, to count the years that had passed since that decision. She was twenty-eight now, and Elena nearly thirty. Their mother kept living. Needing them more these days than ever before.

Sometimes Sam thought that moment, when they were teenagers, on the sofa in the living room behind the curtain Elena had tacked to the ceiling for privacy, had in fact been the best chance to go. She thought of it when the passengers didn't tip, when the water was rough, or when the boat was delayed. But then she thought again. Time had proved Elena's plan right. They couldn't have left without their mother—who would've cared for her, what would she have done?—and their mother, especially as she got sicker, did not want to go. Barring doctors' appointments, she spent most days in bed, as comfortable as possible in the home where she'd raised her children. They would've tried to take her away from that? Convinced her to sell the property and start over somewhere else? It wasn't possible. It could never have been.

So those thoughts, when they came to Sam, were wrong. Elena had been clear. Their only hope was an inheritance. Five hundred thousand dollars, Elena had guessed of the property's value that night in the living room. Half a million in land sitting underneath them. One day it would be in the sisters' names, and then, at last, the ascension that their grandmother had surely expected for their family—an end to the service sector, to split shifts, to suffering—would come to pass. They'd take their final trip across the channel.

Until then, Sam rode the ferry, and brewed strangers' drinks, and filled out surveys about her age and ethnicity and tastes in television. More hours wasted, more anchors dropped. More paychecks earned, deposited, and taken.

Sam was waiting for her life to change. She had spent a long time waiting.

Concessions closed for the evening at eight-thirty. Sam, after locking up, went out to the passenger deck to pass the rest of her ride back to Friday Harbor in rare open air. The islands that swept by were soft and dark with leaves. The sun wouldn't set for another half hour, but the sky was already getting dusky. Crowds were thin. A handful of tourists worn out from their long day at the tide pools.

Down the way, the orange tip of a cigarette glowed over someone's mouth, and though Sam was supposed to intervene (smoking was forbidden on Washington State ferries), she stood there and smelled it. Secondhand pleasure. The thin, delicious breath, the tastes exhaled. Sam used to smoke but she'd had to quit after the state kept raising the price—

ten dollars a pack was unaffordable. A few times after that, she'd bummed smokes off passengers, but then someone complained to a supervisor. All Sam could hope to do now was this: stand with her back to the boat's wet white wall, inhale, and watch the water.

A shape broke the surface. A creature. Moving. Someone near her shouted.

"YOU WON'T BELIEVE WHAT WE SAW FROM THE BOAT tonight," she told Elena, who was at the sink washing the day's dishes. It was late, and Elena's shift had ended hours earlier, but she always waited up for Sam. Elena had brought home from the golf club leftover chili con carne, and Sam was picking at it, shredded cheddar and green onion. Their mother was in her room sleeping. "Will you guess?"

The woods around their house were silent and black. Thick with hawthorn, which grew dark fruit, and Douglas fir. A yellow gleam at the edge of the kitchen window marked the presence of their closest neighbors, the Larsens, who had spotlights tastefully illuminating their landscaping, and who gave too-polite greetings to the girls whenever they bumped into each other in town. Danny Larsen, their youngest son, had asked Elena to homecoming senior year. His mother shut that down immediately.

Elena said, "A dead body."

"Oh, Jesus," Sam said. Put down her fork. "Would I talk like this if we saw a body?"

"I don't know. You get worked up over the weirdest stuff." Elena pushed her hair from her cheek with one wet wrist. "A whale."

"We see whales all the time. Guess again."

"A sea lion."

Sam rolled her eyes. And though she was behind her sister's back, Elena couldn't see her, Elena still seemed to know. The movement must have been felt. So Elena was already on to the next guess: "A merman."

"You're never going to get it. A bear!"

"No way."

"A huge bear! Swimming in the channel!"

Sam had seen it herself: the wet, furred hump of the animal's back, the line of its neck, its pointed nose and small round ears. The water was silver and the sky was dimming blue, and the creature, against those colors, was a dark spot, but the last light in the air outlined its form, made it clear and shocking and strange. The tourists called out to each other in delight. Exclamations in English, Spanish, Chinese. One of them tossed something in the water toward it, and another passenger scolded them. The ferry chugged on, but for a few minutes, long odd ones, the boat and the bear were side by side, pushing forward, abandoning the mainland together, heading out toward the night. The captain even made an announcement over the intercom so anyone sitting inside could come see for themselves. The bear's lifted head. Its slicked shoulders. The widening ripples it left behind. It did not look in their direction as it paddled determinedly on.

Elena was drying the plates now, stacking them in the cupboards. "Where in the channel? You don't think it could reach us, do you?"

"Between Shaw and Lopez." Sam was tickled by the question. "Why? Are you scared?"

"Of bears?"

"Of scary bears?"

"You're not?"

"No way." What was Sam afraid of? Withering away here. Dreaming of chances she'd never be able to take, and shriveling up from that denial, getting poorer and put under more pressure and pushed even farther from the rest of the world. Compared to those fears, getting mauled by a bear seemed a delight.

Elena turned back to the sink. "Our brave girl."

"How was your day?"

"Fine. No wildlife. Unless you count Bert Greenwood coming in drunk at noon."

"That's not unusual, I guess."

"More of a whale than a bear," Elena said.

Her hands were under the faucet. Her face was tipped down, making her neck stretch long and the bones bump up at her nape. "Want me to do the pots?" Sam asked.

Elena shook her head. "It's no problem. Keep talking."

Sam was out of stuff to say. Those few wet minutes see-ing the strange swimmer in the sound had been the only novel ones in the day. Everything else was routine: dismis-sive passengers, weak coffee, stacks of paper cups swaying as the ferry churned on. Except—"Ben asked if I wanted to go camping with him."

Elena looked over her shoulder. Thin and dark as the skin under her eyes was, she still looked, for the moment, bright. Pleased. Like she'd heard a joke. "Camping?"

It was so embarrassing. "On Orcas on Thursday."

"Where? At Moran?"

"At . . . I don't know, I didn't ask."

Elena smirked, just a flash of it, before facing the sink again. "You should go."

"No. Ew," Sam said.

"What's ew about it?"

"I'm not going to spend the night with him. In some tent, stargazing."

"Why not?" Elena was faced away, but Sam could hear the smile in her voice, the little laughter there. "He likes you. It's adorable. He wants to roll up in sleeping bags and make s'mores."

"Don't make fun of me."

Elena turned back around. Her face was sincere. "I'm not making fun of you." A swoop of purple underlining each wide eye. Sam didn't say anything, but she forgave Elena, immediately, with no grudge held, and Elena knew it. "I wouldn't," Elena said. Then returned to the dishes.

"Anyway, I told him no," Sam said. "It's a stupid idea. I'm sure one of us will have to work on Friday."

"So what, you can't board from Orcas?"

Sam didn't know about that, whether she and Ben could start their respective shifts from a different port. But she said, "No. You can't. Anyway, you need me here overnight."

"It's fine." Elena was scrubbing the bottom of a pot. One shoulder high with the effort. "You don't really get up with her anyway."

"Yes, I do," Sam said.

Sudsy water sloshed into the sink. Elena turned on the faucet again, rinsed the pot, and set it on the counter.

This was love: the two of them in the kitchen at the end of the day. The one bond that would last their whole lives. Speaking shorthand, getting irritated, understanding each other so well that they didn't even need to speak the words of a fight out loud.

Sam shook her head at her sister's back. "I can't believe you're sticking up for camping. What a waste of time."

Her sister was rinsing out the empty sink. "Oh, yeah, your precious time."

"I'm not trying to go on dates with Ben. Right? We're not here to get into relationships or whatever." Sam was repeating what Elena herself had said, in so many words, when they were starting high school and things began to get bad with their mother's boyfriend. That man had wanted to set himself up as king. Rule their household. It had been their family's very worst time—no matter how punishing the relentless routine of these days now could feel, they were nothing compared to the actual punishments he had dealt out, his shouting and his hands. Surviving his reign made everything clear: they could only count on each other.

Elena turned off the faucet. "Just saying. A little stargazing sounds like fun."

From the back room, a cough. Sound traveled too easily through this house. Thin walls with meager insulation. Elena took up a dish towel.

"I've got it," Sam said. She put the chili in the fridge and fetched a clean glass from the cupboard. To fill the glass at the sink, she had to stand close to her sister. She put her hand on Elena's back. That touch, and the water glass, were an apology. Elena was right: Sam did not take her fair share of the nighttime responsibilities. Sam could do better. Look at her now, standing, acting. Under her fingertips, Elena's long shoulder blade felt flat as a dish. The water ran over the glass's sides and Elena shut it off.

The sisters were born thirteen months apart. They had been raised together here in their mother's rangy care, in this house that smelled of mildew, where the cupboards were never empty but the utility bills weren't always paid. The men who'd sired them had left long before Sam could remember. Elena said she didn't remember, either. Their mother must have remembered, but had chosen never to tell. When they were young, the girls tried to question her, but she would only distract them in response. If she was painting their nails, they took that quiet moment, her bent worshipful head, as their opportunity to ask: who were their fathers? How'd she meet them? Where'd they go? She would hold up the sisters' hands and say, "Look what a beautiful color you chose." Ice blue with white sparkles for Elena's manicure. Deep, brilliant red for Sam's.

As children, Sam and Elena imagined fathers worthy of keeping secret. Heroes. Princes. Spies gone deep under-cover. But eventually they realized (their mother's boy-friend, when he moved in, proved it) that people refused to speak not about exceptional romantic adventures but about run-of-the-mill assholes. At fourteen and fifteen, the sisters were told by their mother not to complain about their home life. He was stressed, she said, and that's why he lashed out. They all had to be more sympathetic. When Elena mentioned to her tenth-grade science teacher what was going on, and child services got involved, their mother was shocked, silent. Bewildered by their decision to disclose. The social workers visited, wrote up reports, and vanished, and Elena's teacher did nothing after that but gaze with fur-rowed eyebrows at the girls in the school halls. Once the man moved out, no one ever wanted to mention him again. Sam and Elena understood, then, that whoever their fathers were, they were better not discussed.

Their mother hadn't dated anybody seriously since. As kids, the sisters thought they might one day marry—maybe a pair of brothers, they told themselves—and move out, but that didn't happen. Within a couple years, their mother got sick, and so the stories they made up with each other shifted. A town where they were strangers to their neighbors. A garden of their own with two rosebushes, white and red, that they would have the time to indulge in tending.

The dreaming helped. It had since they were children, wondering about the answers to the questions no adults in their life would address. It helped them make sense of what they could not, in everyday life, fathom. When they were teens and their house became unbearable, they went out into the woods, so they could lie on the cool earth between hemlock trees and imagine being elsewhere. Needles shivered over them. Meteors streaked across the sky. The moon, when it was full, was a hole in the darkness, an open door to another world.

These days, they had less time to whisper about what would be. They needed to dedicate their days to what was. But Sam still dreamed. Even over the last two winters, when the days were short and dark, and they were worried about how the virus might threaten their mother, and their existence was so constrained by the pandemic's rules—even then. Sam would stare out her bedroom window to the jumbled constellations. She imagined the moon filled, beyond its white shining surface, with roses. She dreamed, and carried those dreams, precious things, back to Elena to sustain them.

"Thank you, baby," their mother said when Sam handed

her the water. Under the worn cotton of her shirt, her chest
catheter made unnatural lines. "Is your sister up?"

"She's finishing the dishes."

"Would you ask her to come here when she's done?"

Sam said, "Do you need something, Mom?"

"Elena can help me," their mother said.

"I can. More oxygen?"

Their mother hesitated. The water in the glass shivered
in her grip. Finally, she said, "I have to use the toilet."

"Okay."

"I'm sorry. I just need a hand. I'm worn out tonight."

"That's fine. I can do it."

"But don't be rough."

"I'm not," Sam said. "I won't." She stretched out her
fingers, clenched two fists, let them go. She could be the
gentle one.

She drew the blanket off her mother's legs and guided
her feet to the floor. Held one arm around her mother's
waist, helped her stand. Her mother inhaled. The sound
was strained. Sam loosened her grip on her mother's body.
They moved together to the hall, to the bathroom. Sam
knelt, helped her mother with her underwear, and pushed
to get her positioned on the toilet seat.

"Too fast," her mother said.

"What?"

"Slow down."

Sam's muscles were tight with the energy she wasn't ex-
pending. She moved more slowly. Got her mother sitting

where she ought to be. Sat back on her shins on the powdery yellow tile of the bathroom floor.

Her mother, hunched forward, looked at her. The bending over made her breath shorter. She had Elena's deep-set eyes, heavy eyelids, pale hair, and Sam's mouth. She had split herself up, divided her own face, to make them.

"How was work?" she asked.

"Oh," Sam said. "Fine."

They were quiet. Then her mother said, "You think I should be in diapers."

Sam said, "No, I don't. Why do you say that?"

"It wouldn't be easier?"

"I'm pretty sure they're expensive. Would it be easier for you? Do you want them?"

"I can do this by myself," she said. "I do it when you two aren't here. I'm fine."

Recently, their mother smelled, was wet, sometimes when they got home. Elena changed her sheets daily. Sam said, "All right." Her shinbones pressed two hard lines against the tile.

Sam thought about the water off the sides of the ferry. The white pattern of ripples on top, and the bear's bulk breaking through, pushing past. The tree-covered hills that met them at every return to the island. The swaying masts of the hundreds of sailboats moored. She thought about the girls she and Elena went to school with. The few who had stayed; the many who'd left. Their homes vacant during breaks while their families vacationed in Hawaii or at resorts in Mexico. Their manicures done by Sam and Elena's mother for special occasions: nails buffed, cuticles pushed back, formaldehyde and dibutyl phthalate inhaled over hours and weeks and decades. Those girls, turned women, passing occasionally through the golf club with their parents, not bothering to ask Elena how her mother's lungs were. Elena's hands in the sink. The seals barking at the foot of the docks in the harbor.

"Tissue," their mother said. "Please and thank you."

Sam braced her, pulled at her clothes, tried again to move more considerately. When she flushed the toilet, Elena called, "Everything okay?" Yes, Sam called back, don't worry. She escorted their mother to her bed.

That night, Sam woke up to groaning. Elena was in their mother's bedroom talking too low to distinguish the words. Sam didn't want to get up. She knew she should, but she didn't want to—she decided to get up and then the oxygen concentrator turned on and Elena's voice faded and it seemed that everything was fine. Sam listened and in the listening fell back asleep. She dreamed about the woods.

She woke up once more after that—more noises. The sun wasn't up yet, but she had already slept long enough that the first ferry of the day had to be running. That wasn't Sam's business, though. She wasn't working until the afternoon.

The noise wasn't her family, this time. Sounds from outside, scratching, snuffling. An animal on the move.

She rolled over. Her bedroom was so dark that she

couldn't see the dresser or door. It was like her eyes were
shut already. If the bear had swum the channel at this hour,
they would've never seen it—it would've gone by them
shadowed and sleek as a fish. She closed her eyes, black on
black, while thinking of that: the animal. The luck she'd
had to spot it. Sam did feel lucky, sometimes. She did see
some beautiful things.

HAIR WASHED AND JACKET ON, SAM LEFT THE HOUSE at lunchtime and found, damp with the day's drizzle, a heap of speckled feces. She frowned down. A pile on the short path between the road and their front door. Danny Larsen was halfway up his driveway with his big blond dog, and she shouted after him, "Thanks."

Danny turned around. The dog barked and circled his legs. "What?" he yelled back.

Sam shook her head. She turned her car keys over one finger. Not enough for their neighbors to treat them like shit; they had to leave literal piles of the stuff, too. The air stank like meat, musk, hair. A primal stink. Her throat tightened around it. Danny and the dog were making their way toward her.

"Were you talking to me?" Danny asked when he got close enough. The dog bounded back and forth on his driveway. Its plush yellow hair bounced with the movement.

Sam pointed down. "This you?"

"No." Then he had the audacity to smile at her. "I usually use a toilet."

"Your dog," she said. "Is this your dog?"

For one irritating moment, she thought he might respond the same way—my dog's not a big piece of spotted shit, my dog's right here, see?—but he only shook his head, still smiling. "Nope."

Did he think she was stupid? "Who else walks their dog here?" she asked. "It's you."

"That's not from a dog," he said. "A horse, maybe. It's huge."

She bit her cheeks to stop herself from speaking more: oh, what an expert he was, wow. Danny squinted at her. The rain beaded softly on his beard. In high school, he'd been moderately popular, a decent athlete. A kid who acted like he got along with everyone but who followed through with no one. There'd only been three hundred students in the whole school, which made it a tiny, gossipy hellhole, a bucket of crabs snapping at each other and falling over themselves. Sam had to keep her vision focused, on her sister and on graduation, in order to make it through. But there, in her peripheral vision, had been Danny Larsen, carrying his soccer and wrestling and baseball gear, chatting up their teachers, and laughing with classmates.

It infuriated her at the time. He and his pals—their whole cohort. The kids who breezed along as if nothing could ever hurt them. Danny went off to college and returned a couple years later to work for his father's landscaping company. Then his father stepped back, and Danny took over. Now he was a proper businessman. He had a truck with the Larsen name on it, branded T-shirts, and lawn signs advertising his services. He was exactly the same as he'd always been: muscled and friendly and fake.

Sam would rather be honest and solitary than false and surrounded by admirers. She preferred that a thousand times over. Elena was the same way. Sam still couldn't believe Danny had ever tried to date Elena. It was impossible to imagine the two of them even having a conversation.

"You have voles?" he asked. When she didn't respond right away, because he didn't make sense to her, he gestured toward the house. She turned to look. It didn't clarify anything: small, shabby, and cream-colored, as usual. Weeds grew in clumps at its base.

"What?" she said.

"Something's been digging there."

She blinked, then, and noticed at last. The siding beside the front door was damaged. One strip of vinyl, knee-high, had peeled off entirely, and the wood below was gouged.

"Goddamn it," she said. "How long has it been like that?" She was asking herself, really, but Danny shrugged in response.

"Have you noticed any tunnels in the lawn?" he asked. "Voles are wild diggers. They can gnaw through trees. We can help, if you want. They're little but they're a real pest."

The dog's breath was heavy. Simply the sound of it

overwhelmed. Dogs and rodents and—horses, according to Danny—infesting this property, making a zoo of it, attempting to destroy the hope Sam and Elena had left. "Awesome," she said. "Fantastic news, I'm so glad you stopped by."

The corners of Danny's mouth drew in. Keeping the same cordial voice, though, he said, "You called me over."

"Right," she said. "Well. Thanks for pointing that out."

They both stood there. She had to get to the ferry terminal. Her shift started at three. At Sam's feet lay the wet, coiled stool.

"How's your mom doing?" Danny asked. "And your sister?"

"Fine. Both of them."

"I actually don't think I've seen your mom in a couple weeks. She's okay?"

"She's fine," Sam said again. "She just . . . she's not very mobile. She gets dizzy when she stands for too long."

"Sorry to hear that. You all are looking for a different doctor for her? You go to Boyce right now?"

"Oh," Sam said. "I guess. I don't know. That's more Elena's idea. Mom says she likes Dr. Boyce."

"Just in case, I gave Elena the name of the clinic my parents go to. Their specialists are in Mount Vernon. They really like it."

Mount Vernon, a long ferry ride away. Two hours, in total, once you added the drive—they'd have to take a full day off work. All that to accompany their mother to a single appointment, where they would sit in a waiting room for ages before getting the exact same diagnoses she already had: sarcoidosis, pulmonary hypertension, interstitial lung disease. The same suggestions to enroll in clinical trials she couldn't access. The same offerings of treatments they could barely afford, and that wouldn't fix anything, anyway. Diuretics, digoxin, inhaled oxygen. Everything designed to distract from what their mother herself had long said was inevitable: she was going to die from this.

"Thanks," Sam said.

The dog shoved forward against Danny's pant leg to sniff the foul air between them. Danny stroked its soft back, held it in place. "If you ever need anything," he added.

"We're good."

"But if you do," he said. "I told your sister the same thing. We're just down the road."

Sam could perfectly picture him ordering the chili at one of Elena's tables and offering his assistance. He was so annoying. And he forced her into pretense right along with him—that was one of his worst qualities, that his niceness could make Sam feel like she ought to play nice, too. "I have to get to work," she said, "but it was good catching up with you, Danny."

He gestured to the ground. "Want me to pick that up? I have bags."

No, she wanted to say, get off this property, stop talking to my sister, stay away from my family's pain. The notion of a popular kid scraping waste off their walkway was too appealing, though. She said, "That'd be great. Thanks."

Behind them, the side of the house lay open, a line of its innards exposed.

The rain got heavier that afternoon. From the ferry, Sam watched drops track across the windows, waves slosh on the horizon. The boat swayed. She braced herself against the counter. When she had to go help a customer at the tea station, boiling water splashed on her wrist, and the customer apologized and she apologized, too, furious with herself and everyone around her. Afterward she took an apple juice from the beverage fridge to press against her burning skin.

The sun was down by the time she got home. Their woods were silhouetted against the sky. The light above their front door was on, so she could see that the pile was gone. Rain had washed the ground where it once lay, but hadn't gotten rid of the smell entirely.

She pushed her key into the front door's lock, trying not to let her jacket sleeve rub against the tender pink blotch on her wrist. She was moving slowly. Next to the steps, where the siding was missing, was a spot of raw wood made dark by the wet air. Parallel lines of splinters ran along it.

She eased open the lock. Inside the house was Elena's voice and their mother's blaring television set. That stink was all around still, smelling like stomach acid and gaping bodies, like soggy fur and an unwashed mouth. Sour and rotten. Copper and earth. "Took you long enough," Elena called from the living room, and Sam let herself inside.

THEY WOKE THE NEXT DAY TO A BEAR AT THE DOOR.

WHEN THE SISTERS WERE YOUNG, VERY YOUNG, THEY loved living on San Juan. Summers, the girls would go over to Lime Kiln and pass entire days posted up on the rocky bluffs watching for whales. Spotting them was like catching shooting stars. You couldn't focus on any one spot—you had to let your gaze go wide. Elena was especially good at it. She would jostle Sam's elbow and say, "Humpback." The tourists next to them, outfitted with binoculars, gasped, leaning close to try to learn her secrets. Elena pointed out the pods. Humpbacks, gray whales, minkes, porpoises rolling and leaping in the surf. Gorgeous orcas, with their dorsal fins sharp as blades.

The girls hiked along the coastal cliffs as otters floated below. They went north, to English Camp, where a Coast Salish longhouse once stood, and played pretend among the thick damp ferns. Park rangers waved in their direction. Elena asked where they came from, what they did here, whether they liked it, and they told her the names of their hometowns and the list of their duties and how, yes, they treasured this place. Sam and Elena chased each other down the park's trails. They hooted and squealed. Their world seemed enchanted, a paradise.

They pulled out grass in clumps below people's fences and fed it to the farm animals trapped behind: cows with wide wet eyes and luxurious lashes; sheep with flat, shocked human-seeming faces; long-necked alpacas who teetered over to them on thin legs. They watched the buzzing activity around neighbors' bee boxes and pictured honey heists where they would crack a box open and steal its combs. Overhead, bald eagles held tight to tree branches. When roosters crowed, the sisters crowed back.

Blackberries and salmonberries grew wild in the bushes. Stained the girls' fingers, their mouths. On the island's south tip, in American Camp, they walked through grasses as tall as they were, where soft white flowers brushed their cheeks and ears. Tiny, rare marbled butterflies floated by. Foxes emerged on the paths ahead and stared, bold as could be, before vanishing into the undergrowth.

Even school, back then, seemed like an adventure. Or at least it wasn't yet a site of social torture. Sam liked her teachers, up until third grade or so. She didn't mind her classmates. She enjoyed the activities. They had pancake breakfasts; they skimmed pages at book fairs; they even, one year, got to spend three days aboard an enormous sailboat to learn about the marine ecosystem of the Salish Sea. In those contexts, Sam's lack of friends didn't matter. The school programmed their days, filling them with fun, so none of the students bothered to spend time on who was fitting in and who wasn't. Or at least Sam didn't bother. She poured syrup, flipped through chapters, gaped at Steller sea lions, and generally busied herself with the fantasy that she already had everything she could ever want or need.

The girls' playgrounds were the stacks of driftwood on the beach. Deer peered at them from the hills. The sisters hid behind bleached logs and called out to each other. They stacked sticks to make shelters, then crouched inside. They dangled seaweed, salt-smelling, from their fingertips.

Did they know, then, how little their family had, and how precarious their grip on that little bit was? They had no idea. Each evening, their mother came home from the salon exhausted. Stinking of solvents. Sometimes she would cough. But the girls didn't know yet—none of them knew—that the chemicals she inhaled were growing granulomas in her lungs, causing her lymph nodes to swell, narrowing her arteries. Their mother made them scrambled eggs or buttered noodles for dinner. She poured vegetables onto their plates. Canned peas, canned beets, canned corn. They told her what they'd seen on the island that day, and she oohed and aahed, making them proud as young queens.

Their power went out some days in winter. Elena rubbed their mother's shoulders in front of the TV. The sisters crouched on the forest floor on their property, studying mushrooms, telling each other stories. They were heroines. They made magic. They were the girls at the center of a fairy tale, and they, along with their mother, would live in such bliss all their days.

This was not a fairy tale. They were not, faced with this beast on their step, brave. Sam woke up to the shock of a door slamming and Elena's scream. Hearing the tumult, Sam knew immediately, horribly, that Elena had found their mother dead. Sam had been bracing for that moment for years but still it knocked her heart out of her chest. She couldn't breathe, couldn't think. She tumbled out of bed, hit the floor with both feet, and ran.

Elena was in the front hall shaking. Sam was shaking, too, by then, coursing with dread and adrenaline, trying to prepare for whatever it was they would have to do. Their mother. Their anchor. "Where is she?" Sam said.

"There's a bear."

From behind her bedroom door, their mother was calling. "Elena?"

Sam couldn't adjust. "She—"

"A fucking bear," Elena said. "Oh my god." She pressed her hands to her face, covered her eyes. Her trembling fingers stretched to her hairline, threading under the blond strands. "It's right outside."

Their mother's door opened. She was repeating their names. Sam said, "There's a what?"

"There's a *bear*." Elena took her hands down. "What do we do?"

"What do we—" Sam didn't understand. Her rational mind hadn't woken up yet, so the situation seemed incomplete, incomprehensible. She wanted to sit on the floor and have someone explain it to her. But Elena was hysterical. Turning to face their mother, Sam said, "Everything's okay."

"What happened?" their mother asked. "She's hurt?" Her fists were pressed to her chest. The collar of her shirt was low enough to expose the top of her catheter. Her sternum, pale and ridged with bone.

"Everyone's fine. Right?" Sam looked to Elena, who kept shaking. Turned back to their mother. "We're fine. Elena just got a fright."

Their mother didn't understand, either. "What happened?"

"She got scared. Something outside."

"There's a *bear outside*," Elena said.

"A what!" exclaimed their mother. "No!"

"We're going to take care of it," Sam said. To their mother, but to Elena, too, and to herself, because she did need assurance, she couldn't clear the awful vision of their mother found stiff in bed, their mother gone from them. She went over to hold their mother's thin arm. It was cool but not cold—not yet. "Don't worry. We'll call the police."

"Animal control," their mother said.

"Animal control," Sam agreed. She squeezed their mother's arm, and their mother squeezed back, pulling Sam's hand toward her for a second, showing Sam she was still here. Sam said, "Go rest."

As soon as their mother was back in her room, Sam said, quick, "What are you talking about, a bear?"

They went together to the window in the living room. Elena was holding on to Sam now. Sam could feel her quaking, the tendons seizing, Elena's effort over and over to release them and how they refused. "Be careful," Elena whispered. But Sam, having seen their mother, wasn't scared anymore. It wasn't that she didn't trust her older sister, or didn't heed sincere warnings, or didn't fear apex predators—she simply couldn't process how it was possible, an animal like that outside. Here? The words made no sense. Had the ferry story made Elena delusional? She, who had spent her whole adulthood so levelheaded? Yet there was her movement, the seize and release, at Sam's side.

And there, Sam saw through the glass, was a bear.

It was hunkered down at their front door, just at the edge of the walkway. It faced away. Its rump was huge, thickly furred, gold and black and brown. Matted in spots. Dense with texture. Past that, the lump of its shoulders, the soft half circles of its small high ears. Its head was massive. It turned its face and the sisters shrank from the window. But it was calm. It looked in profile toward the road, sniffed the air, and yawned, expansive, a mouth opening vastly, yellow teeth exposed three inches long, black lips curling back and tongue spilling forth. It shut its mouth and faced away from them again.

"Is this real?" Elena whispered. Her warm breath against Sam's cheek.

Sam stared. The smudged windowpane, the cracking

frame—the slimmest of barriers between them and it. There, not ten feet away, was the animal's massive body. As big as three men. Wider, stronger, and far deadlier. Its tail, its back, its thighs. It twitched and its muscles rippled. A dark stripe of fur lay over its spine.

Elena clung to her. Sam said they had to call someone. Get help.

The 911 operator told them to calm down and breathe. They described the animal outside. Clutching Sam's phone, they talked while pressed against the refrigerator. The bear, with a blow, could smash through one of their windows, barge into the kitchen, demolish their lives, but they huddled there as if the humming fridge could protect them. From the back of the house, their mother made a sound, and Elena met Sam's eyes. Grimaced. The operator told them someone would be there soon.

After they hung up, they listened. All Sam could hear were the rustles of Elena's body: her lips parting, her throat working. There was nothing from outside. A long minute passed. Elena said, "I'm going to check on Mom."

Once she was alone, Sam realized that she was still in her pajamas—a T-shirt and underwear. Elena, who got up earlier on the days Sam worked the late shift, was already dressed, but Sam was bare-legged, half-naked, and goosebumped. She needed to put pants on. But she was afraid to leave her post at the front of the house. Step by cautious step, she crept out to the living room and peeked through the edge of the window. It was still there. Sitting fat and relaxed. She backed away and hurried to her room.

While she was pulling on a pair of leggings, she heard her sister whispering. "Sam?" Sam hopped over to her bedroom door. Elena was coming down the hall. When she saw Sam, she collapsed her shoulders, performing relief: "Oh, God, I thought you might've gone out there."

"Out *there*?"

"I don't know!"

Sam adjusted her waistband and came to Elena's side. "She's okay?"

"She's fine." They kept whispering to each other. Did bears have good hearing? Like owls? Sam had no idea. Elena said, "Why'd it come here?"

Sam couldn't begin to guess. She had the urge, then, to go back to the living room, to check. "Is it still outside?"

"I mean, we didn't hear it leave."

Sam eased along the hall. Elena followed. They went together to the front. Together, it was easier to be brave; Sam knew Elena was worried, but that worry wrapped around them both like a shield, making it easier to step forward, easier to move. Sam got to the window's edge, and yes, there it was, its brown fur bright in the sun. The sisters had seen whales, plenty of times, and cattle, but Sam could not wrap her mind around the size of this particular thing—the bear's proximity threw off her sense of scale. Its head alone . . . the width of its neck. She took out her phone. Tried to get a picture. Couldn't fit it all in the frame.

Elena said, "Be careful."

"I'm being careful," Sam whispered back.

On her screen, it looked like a lump, a badly folded shag rug. Sam took the pictures anyway. She needed to have the record. It was too strange. The photos were terrible, though. Her phone's camera kept focusing on the smudged glass of the window, making the bear, beyond it, a blur. Sam came closer to the pane.

The bear moved. It rose to all fours, shifting its weight, and shivered. A cloud of sunlit dust rose off.

Elena yanked her back. Hissed, "Jesus Christ." Sam's heart was knocking in her chest again, smashing against the container of her rib cage. They pulled each other to the kitchen, where they huddled, waiting for rescue.

It took nearly half an hour for anyone to arrive. Long enough that their heart rates fell, and they got bored, there against the fridge, and Sam remembered all over again the uselessness of asking for help from the authorities. How many times in their lives had they been let down?

Sam took out her phone and opened a survey. "Send me those pictures," Elena said, and Sam did. Elena texted her manager to say she'd be late, then texted the other server about getting there earlier to cover. The phone buzzed in Elena's palm. Elena showed Sam her screen: *Stop playing,* her co-worker had written back, followed by three fat-cheeked brown bear emojis. Sam was struck by how insufficient those cartoon images were. As the flat-faced blond princess emoji was to Elena—a cap of hair, a thin smile, a golden crown—these blobby, even-keeled teddy bears were to the creature outside. The thing at their door was something more complicated, more volatile, than those could even hint at. It had capacities they could not imagine.

Elena kept texting. Sam tapped her way through two surveys and started a third.

At last, a knock on the door. Elena jumped, and then laughed, too loud, covering her mouth. Sam had to laugh along. The sound was high. Shrieky. "I thought it was the bear," Elena said.

"I know. Me too."

Impossible as that was, the beast rising to its hind legs, brushing itself off, smoothing the fur back from its brow with one monstrous paw, and giving three sharp raps to the door, Sam and Elena moved forward fearfully. They turned the lock and the knob. The door pushed toward them, and Sam, by instinct, pushed back, trying to defend her family, before she absorbed that there were two people on the step. A human hand reaching out.

"Sheriff's office," one of the two uniformed men said. "You called about a wildlife disturbance?"

The sisters explained. Sam started, then Elena stepped in to give the morning's details. Sam took out her phone, the pictures, to show its shape, its bulk. The golden brown richness. The breadth of its body. The air between them stank of musk.

One sheriff's deputy was taking notes. The other stepped off their walkway to look at the ground, the dirt and trampled weeds.

"And you're sure it wasn't a deer," the note-taking one said. "Maybe a mama and a baby. Curled up together so they looked big."

"No, this was— Absolutely not," Elena said.

Sam said, "We got a good look at it. It was right here."

The deputy kept writing. The other one said, "Does with their young can be very aggressive."

"It wasn't a deer," Elena said.

The note-taking one took their names and phone numbers. He confirmed their address. He asked them how long they'd been there, and if they'd ever seen anything like this before.

Finally he clicked the top of his pen and threaded it through the coils at the top of his notebook. "What we're going to do," he said, "is report this to the Washington Department of Fish and Wildlife. Someone from there might reach out to you to follow up. But this isn't unheard of. We had one swim over from Whidbey a couple years ago. You girls remember that?"

Sam and Elena shook their heads.

"They island-hop on their way to Canada."

"One of the world's largest black bear populations over there," the other deputy said.

"Oh, really?" said Elena, faint and polite.

"Believe it," the formerly note-taking deputy said. "Vancouver Island. So in our experience, so long as it's not bothering anyone, not getting into garbage or chasing your pets or anything, we leave it be, let it make its way west. It's on the move anyway."

"You can give us a call if you see it again," the second deputy added.

"Keep us posted," the first one said. "So we can track it. No need to approach it, no need to shoot at it—"

"Shoot at it," Sam repeated.

"For example," the other deputy said. "Not suggesting you two would, but some guys, you know, get it into their heads to try."

"We just hid," Elena said.

"Well, good," said the deputy. He gave them his card. Told them they could contact the public records office to get a copy of their case report if they wanted. Reminded them that someone from the WDFW might be in touch. And informed them they had nothing to worry about.

Behind the deputies and the green-striped car marked as a nonemergency vehicle, the woods were lush and shadowed. Oak leaves brushed against each other in the morning breeze. Birds called. The bear was out there somewhere. It was moving, heavy, between the trees, its claws sinking into the soil. It had visited them and then moved on to its next destination, wherever that might be.

It must have been the same bear Sam saw from the ferry, though the officers had made it sound as though these animals made a routine of crossing the sound. But really, that couldn't be true, she'd been working on the boat for years and never seen such a thing. Unless the waters had changed somehow during the pause forced by the pandemic . . . but she'd been living on the island all her life, and they'd never had bears, she'd heard stories maybe only once or twice before—she could hardly remember—no one had ever talked about a thing like this.

The sheriff's deputies left. Sam and Elena shut the door, faced each other, and laughed. Loud, glorious. Like they were little kids at play again. How strange—how magical. How grand.

"Girls?" their mother called.

"That was the sheriff," Sam called back. "Everything's fine. It's gone."

"Come and tell me," their mother said.

Elena was still looking at Sam. Elena's expression was radiant, giggly. She was trying to pinch her mouth shut. The corners of her eyes were creased. "I have to get to work," she said.

"I'll drive you," Sam said. "Let me just tell Mom."

"Okay." Elena didn't let her go yet, though; she stood smiling. "That was crazy."

"Insane."

"I was so scared."

"You opened the door and it was there?"

"It was right there," Elena said. Laughing again, awed, thrilled. "Oh my god. What'll I tell everyone?"

"They must be dying for details. Are they still texting you? They probably think it gobbled you up by now."

Elena shook her head. "I can't believe that actually happened."

"I know. No one's going to believe us," Sam said. "Oh, well." Elena grinned at her, and Sam went to get her shoes and car keys.

No ONE ELSE WOULD GET IT, BUT SAM, EVEN AFTER spending the ride to the club reliving the sighting with Elena, couldn't keep the encounter quiet—it was too exciting not to talk about. It made her usual dull routine glow. She had been frightened, absolutely, but now, with the bear gone, the adrenaline in Sam had turned to sheer thrill.

On returning home, Sam hurried to her mother's room, where she refilled her mother's water glass, adjusted her pillows, and took her through every detail. The bear, the wait, the police, the plan. "We're supposed to call in any more sightings," Sam said, and her mother said, seriously, "All right," which made Sam wonder—how often in a day did her mother even look out the window? When she was first diagnosed, the fatigue and shortness of breath were manageable, but as time passed, she spent more and more hours in bed, concentrating her effort on her oxygen intake, metering out the life she had left. All the same, Sam played along, for this short moment, with the story that her mother was an active member of their community, a participant in the wider world outside this house's door. "We need to be careful," Sam said, "until they confirm it's off the island. The sheriff's deputies said it won't hurt us but you never really know."

That afternoon, on the ferry, Sam told one of the deckhands who swung by concessions for a soda. He raised his eyebrows but didn't move his mouth inside his wiry gray beard. Once he left, Sam busied herself by sorting the cash in the register so the bills faced the same way. Presidents looking to starboard. The deckhand hadn't understood; the deputies, that morning, hadn't either. She didn't know why she had bothered telling anybody. It was too bizarre to share.

Then that deckhand returned with another crew member. They asked for the story again. Sam perked right up. She gave them all the details, and free coffees, too.

A few hours later, Ben appeared in her galley. In his yellow reflective vest, he shone through the dinnertime crowd. His radio was looped across his chest. When he caught her looking, he winked. Sam turned to the register and shook her head. A passenger came up to ask her how the sausages were. She shrugged. The passenger trotted off to grab himself one from the rolling rack. Keeping her head bowed, Sam rang up ice creams for two teenagers, bagged nuts for an old man. Gleaming yellow stayed in her peripheral vision. The line cleared, she raised her eyes, and Ben was there.

"So you don't answer any of my texts," he said, "but you pick up the call of the wild?"

Sam tightened her mouth so she wouldn't smile at him. "Don't be dumb."

"Come on. I want to hear."

"What's there to tell?" she said. "It was only a grizzly sitting on our front step. Practically ringing the doorbell."

Ben hadn't been working the evening the bear swam the channel, but he'd heard about it, of course, from the other deckhands. They all gossiped down there in the bowels of the boat. He was newer to the ferry system than Sam was, but he'd started during the pandemic, while dining was closed, so he had months on her of working with these particular people. They were chummy. It reminded Sam, sometimes, of high school. If Ben had been there with her, instead of six hundred miles south smoking weed and driving his parents crazy, he would've sunk right into Friday Harbor's tiny social scene. Been the snarky kid at the back of the classroom, played golf, gotten high with the popular crowd after the last bell rang. He wouldn't have bothered with Sam. And she would've found him annoying. Sometimes she still did. At least, she knew she should.

He leaned over her counter. "Don't you have to work?" she asked, and he said yes, he did, but he didn't move. So she told him the whole thing. He gasped. He goggled. He performed, beautifully, the same amazement that tourists did when a whale surfaced alongside their boat. Sam decided not to mind it this time. When she took out her phone to show him the pictures, he took it from her, and, while a passenger came up to the counter to buy a handful of candy bars, pinched the screen, zooming in. Ben's hair was a cap of brown waves. His neck was long and thin. His ears stuck out. Elena had told Sam, years earlier, not to get distracted by romance, which was an easy guideline to follow when hanging around a guy like him. Sam rang up someone else's bag of chips.

Ben's radio crackled. "I've got to go," he said, handing the phone back. "You're sure you're not up for Orcas to-night?"

"Yeah. I can't."

"You could," he said. "You just don't want to."

Sam shrugged. "Okay, I don't want to." She slipped her phone under the counter. He left for the lower deck, his body a yellow buoy bobbing away.

She sold people chowders, caramel corn, and baked goods. The shift passed more easily than usual. The more Sam spread the story around, the more the bright, busy feeling that had come over her after the bear left seeped into every bit of the day: how big the animal had been, how vivid and close, became, in her retelling, fantastic qualities, exhilarating rather than intimidating. Now that she knew she and Elena were safe, that they had survived it and laughed at the end, she almost wished it would happen again.

Toward the end of her shift, Ben popped up in front of

her counter and growled. Sam jumped and yelped and laughed again. The passengers milling in front of the beverage fridge smiled in confusion. Past the galley windows, the water reflected the white, round, low sun.

It was a wonderful day. When Sam got home after work, she and Elena talked through their morning over again. They reminded each other of the details one had forgotten: the long roll of the animal's tongue, the mound at the top of its back. What Sam had blurted out to the police when they first arrived: "'What else were you doing all this time?'" Elena quoted, delighted at the impropriety. Sam didn't even remember. The deputies' faces had fuzzed into one pale, sandy-haired blot of authority in her mind. She only wanted to talk with Elena about the ferocious thing they'd seen, the dangerous magic they had lived through.

In bed, that night, Sam took surveys while her thoughts wandered. The floorboards in the hall creaked. Her sister came in and crawled onto the covers beside her.

"I can't sleep," Elena whispered.

Sam clicked off her screen and nestled down next to her sister. Their mother's room was silent on the other side of the wall. Sam missed this: the two of them curled up in this bedroom. Telling secrets to each other in the dark.

Sam said, "I wish we'd gotten better pictures of it."

"You should've taken a video."

"I will if it comes back."

"Ooh," Elena said. They lay there. The long weight of

Elena's body held Sam's covers, so she was pinned, pleasantly, under her sheet. Warm and secure. Exhaustion hit her like a blow. Her jaw and eyes ached.

Elena kept talking, steady. "I didn't think it was real when I first saw it. I used to have nightmares about that. A bear."

Sam unstuck her mouth. "No, you didn't."

"Yes, I did," Elena said. "When we were kids, I'd have dreams that we were outside and a bear, or sometimes a wolf, would try to get us. And I'd have to save you and Mom."

That wasn't true, Sam thought. At least, she didn't remember them—these nightmares. She remembered Elena dreaming about sharks. Sharks? Or was it—an octopus? Elena was scared, even now, of deep water—not being able to see her feet under the surface—murkiness—Elena was still talking. It was too much to listen. Swaddled in her sister's voice, by the hush of her meaningless words, Sam let herself, happily, drift.

THEIR ENCOUNTER WAS COVERED IN THE SAN JUAN *Journal,* bolstered by quotes from the sheriff's office and a state biologist. Over the week that followed, the newspaper reported two more sightings: one a few miles from them, by False Bay, and one up by Cabbage Leaf Inn. It printed blurry pictures of a furred animal photographed from a distance. Soon enough, the bear became to Sam like everything else: a thing laid claim to by other people. Sam and Elena's experience, though the first, closest, and most shocking, faded. Was taken away.

Sam and Elena went to work. They tended to their responsibilities. Sam answered enough questions to reach the survey website's redemption threshold of twenty-five dollars, which she would receive as a gift card and put toward the water bill. Then she started over again. When her shifts overlapped with Ben's, he came up to the galley to bug her, and if there weren't any customers, she would take a break from her register, and they would fuck in the bathroom. Inside her, heat bloomed, vivid. She pushed his shirt up and scratched her nails over his back. His radio hissed and crackled. Life went on as usual, until the Friday evening when she got a call, then another, then a text, from her sister. Elena wrote, *Answer.*

The ferry was leaving Shaw Island for Lopez—Sam barely had cell service. She called her sister back right away. Elena was panting on the other end of the line.

"What is it?" Sam said. Startled, distressed. Picturing the worst, of course. Their mother. Elena's quick breath foretold death.

"I saw it again," Elena said. "The bear. It was right next to me."

Passengers were already gathering in front of Sam's counter; announcements were playing through the loudspeakers. Sam was trying to listen, but the call couldn't go on too long. The man closest to her register frowned at her. She grabbed his food—two apples and a cinnamon roll—and rang it up. Handed over his receipt while the phone was pressed to her ear. Elena was talking fast, but more from leftover jitters than any current danger. It seemed like the most fearsome moment was past. Still, Sam made Elena promise to text her, and report it, and stay safe. A passenger was asking a question about the wine selection. Sam had to hang up.

She showed the passenger the drinks on offer. They wanted to know what was local. "They all are," Sam said. They wanted to know which was the most local. If any came from the islands themselves, and if so, where. Sam

picked up the bottles to look at the small print on their la-
bels. Tucked in her back pocket, her cellphone held her
world.

Elena kept texting through Sam's shift, thank God. Sam
propped her phone behind a tower of plastic to-go lids so
she could see the notifications appear on screen while she
worked.

> *On Cattle Point right after the farm*
> *I literally went right by it while I was walking home.*
>   *Maybe forty feet away*
> *Standing in the woods. I froze*
> *No one else was around*
> *It was so calm. Just looking at me. Very big*
>   *and beautiful*
> *I can't wait to tell you*

People kept bringing her their food. Sam rang up Greek
yogurt and draft beer. She counted correct change. The
boat passed out of cellphone range for a long, silent half
hour, and then a shore appeared through the galley windows and the phone vibrated again.

> *The most beautiful yellow eyes*

It wasn't until her shift was over that Sam could call her
sister back. Standing at the ferry's rusty bow, Sam watched

her screen until two bars of cell service appeared. The wind was fresh and wet on Sam's face. Elena picked up. Her breathing on the other end of the line was regular now— she was home, she said, and all was well. Their mother had felt strong enough at dinnertime for them to eat together in the kitchen. Sam said that was good news, and Elena agreed, and then Elena said their mother was in her room resting, and Sam waited for Elena to go on. The edge of San Juan was growing larger on the horizon. The wind kept pushing. Finally, Sam asked Elena to tell her every bit of what had happened.

Elena must have been waiting for the invitation. She rushed right in. She said she had been walking, like normal, back from work, a two-mile commute around the mowed edge of the golf course and then through the private planned community on Fairway Drive and along the trail that bordered Cattle Point Road. That trail, a quiet dirt path that connected the town of Friday Harbor to the visitor center at American Camp, took Elena from home to her job and back every day. It rolled past pasture and woodlands and fenced-off properties. She'd hardly seen anything there more threatening than spiderwebs. This evening, she'd been humming to herself. Her headphones were in and her sneakers treaded softly on the ground. She saw a movement beside her, in the trees, and turned. She expected to see a deer. The bear came out.

"You're kidding," Sam said. Her waist was pressed against the ferry's railing. On the level exposed below her, deckhands were moving, preparing to come into harbor. Passengers drifted. Soon they would be called to their cars.

"Right there in the woods," Elena said. "And looking straight at me." Elena had stopped moving, averted her eyes. She could sense it padding forward.

Elena said she couldn't stop trying to calculate the distance between them. Forty feet? Thirty? A few car lengths—an instant away, she knew, had the bear decided to attack. She held her breath and turned her head slowly in its direction. She saw its paws, which stunned her—their size— Over the phone, she laughed, then. "I'm holding up my hands," she told Sam. "Like you can see me." Its paws were the size of a dinner plate, she said. Bigger than a human skull. Sam pictured her sister's skinny fingers drawing a circle in the air, sketching out the claws that could've killed her.

The bear was losing its light in Sam's memory. It was turning into something shadowed and frightful. "Did you call the sheriff?" Sam asked.

"Sure," Elena said.

"Did they find it?"

"I don't think so."

"How soon did they get there?"

"I don't know," Elena said. "I didn't call them until after. Doesn't it feel kind of silly to call?"

"Silly how?"

"Like . . . what was there to say? The bear left. I saw it leave. We looked at each other and then it kept going into the woods."

This didn't make sense. "They told us to call. They're trying to track it."

"I know," Elena said. She sounded distracted.

Then Elena turned the conversation back to the bear. Describing it, she was focused. Detailed. Reverent, even. She spent a long time talking about its body. The impossibility of its size. The thickness of its arms, the depth of its smell, the force it exuded—its presence had made Elena's ears keener and her eyes sharper, had shocked her senses into new sensitivity. It had looked right at her. Taken her in. Its eyes were small, close-set, colored a rich orangey yellow and lined with black. Its nose twitched as they stood there together. It inhaled her.

Elena talked about her sighting the way a person might if an angel touched down in front of them, or if a burning bush spoke, or if, Sam supposed, a grizzly walked up, met their gaze, and did not do them harm. It was remarkable, certainly. To come so close to danger and emerge unscathed. Elena's day, before seeing it, must have been tedious, spotted by moments of frustration, but after crossing the bear's path, the simple fact of her life had to be recast as some sort of miracle.

The ferry blasted its horn. Sam pressed the phone against her ear. Even through the air-shaking sound, Elena's words came through clear and joyous. Elevated. Alive.

But when she talked about the rest of it—all the details that now seemed more urgent to Sam—she reverted to her usual voice. The most matter-of-fact and unimpressed ver-

sion of herself, actually. When did the police arrive? Had
the animal followed her home? Was she worried about the
walk to work in the future? Elena didn't seem to care.

"You should take the car tomorrow," Sam said. "You'll
just have to drive me to the dock in the morning. I can walk
from town to meet you in the afternoon."

"No, I'm fine," Elena said, breezily. "You take it."

"You can't go on the trail again. Not if you know it's out
there and coming up to people."

"I'm really fine."

"El," Sam said. "Please."

Elena agreed. But she didn't sound scared, and Sam
didn't understand why not. Sam was. During the ferry's
docking routine, as Sam descended to the car deck and Ben,
holding a rope, grinned at her and she stepped off the boat
onto the wooden slats of the pier, she worried about how
close the bear had been.

The week before, at their door, it'd been even closer, but
she'd felt safer, then, separated from it by walls. And she and
Elena had been together. This experience, Elena alone with
it in the woods, nothing but rotten air between them—this
was different.

Sam walked to the car on shaky legs. She could imagine
it, what Elena went through. Heading home, worn out, one
foot ahead of the other on the uneven dirt path, and then
hearing movement. Another body nearby.

The bear stepping out and staring at her. Its small, glowing eyes and enormous wet mouth. Its claws digging into

the earth. If Sam had been in Elena's shoes, she would've screamed, or tried to run, or—anything, not knowing in the least what was right to do. Raised her arms? Climbed a tree? Stood there pissing her pants and weeping, waiting to be chewed apart.

Elena said she'd had nightmares as a child about this. A monster approaching her. She had lived that nightmare now.

The trees. The dirt. Its teeth. Her breath. The horror of that particular dream coming true.

SAM DROVE HOME WITH HER MOUTH DRY AND HER HANDS clenched around the steering wheel. The lights at the front of the house were out when she arrived. Elena wasn't in the kitchen or the living room, so Sam crossed to her mother's bedroom, knocked, and opened the door.

Her mother looked up. The television was on: a show about homicide investigations, with a picture of some pale Elena look-alike on the screen. "Where's El?" Sam asked.

"She's not out there?" her mother said. "Give her a call."

Sam shut her mother's door and dialed Elena. Two long rings sounded before Elena answered.

"You're home already?" Elena said.

"Where are you?"

Elena lowered her voice, trying to be soothing. "I'm taking a walk."

"Okay," Sam said. "Are you serious?"

"I just needed to get out of the house. I was too worked up. Don't freak out, I'm fine, I'm around other people." In the background of the call, a dog barked, as if to prove Elena's point.

Sam understood claustrophobia, she understood the overwhelming tension of having too much on your mind, but she didn't understand taking a stroll in brand-new bear country. Sometimes, as terrible as it was, you needed to stay home. "Where are you? I'll come get you."

"Stay there," Elena said. "I'm close. I'll be back in ten."

It took fifteen. Sam had to be up at three-thirty in the morning—these were the most demanding times on her schedule, going from a late shift one day to an early one the next—so she, after checking in with their mother one last time, started getting ready for bed. She brushed her teeth while looking out at the road from the living room window. At last, she saw Elena coming. Sam spat her toothpaste in the kitchen sink and opened the front door. She called, "Are you insane?"

Elena shook her head. "What are you worried about?"

"Oh," Sam said. "Good question. I don't know. Maybe the fucking grizzly bear?"

Elena was inside by that time. She locked the door after them while Sam shoved the brush back in her mouth. "You know it was totally random, right? My seeing it. It moves all over the place."

Sam popped the brush out. "Seems like it's hanging around here."

"It's probably on Shaw by now."

Sam headed toward the bathroom. Elena followed. With her sister there, Sam did, now, feel a bit more settled. She replaced her brush in the medicine cabinet and rinsed her mouth. Elena's face was behind her in the mirror, and looking amused, still.

Sam turned around. "You're not worried."

Elena smiled wide at her. "No." Sam could see the shine of Elena's teeth. The overlap of her canine that, in nervous moments, Elena used to press against with one finger, in the fruitless hope of pushing it back into place.

"That didn't scare you today?"

"No, it scared the shit out of me," Elena said. "Completely. But once I realized he wasn't going to do anything, it was like . . . well, isn't this cool?" Sam huffed at that. Elena insisted: "Isn't it?"

"I guess," Sam said.

Elena was excited. That sound was still in her voice. Having seen something enormous and raw, she'd been awed. Sam could picture it: her sister the virgin chosen for ritual killing. Danger immediate as a hungry god before her. And yet Elena was unharmed.

Sam had to admit that was pretty cool. Sure. Except: "I don't like how close it's been to the house."

Elena shrugged. "I think we're okay."

Cool mint tingled on the insides of Sam's cheeks, her gums and tongue. "Should we get a dog?"

Her sister laughed.

"For protection," Sam clarified.

"I'm imagining Jessie."

"Who's Jessie?"

"The Larsens' dog," Elena said. "Jessie. You know? All sweet and fluffy, trying to protect us."

"Oh, God," Sam said. That animal couldn't even save itself from its groomer. "Fine. Should we get a gun?"

Elena said, "Sammy, we're okay. I promise."

And empty as that was—what could her sister's words do that a guard dog or hunting rifle couldn't?—Sam was, somehow, comforted. That they would make it through terrifying things, that they would be able to leave with no scars other than the ones they already had. There was no animal lurking. There was no permanent damage to fear. Elena would take care of them, as she always had. They would take care of each other.

THE PHONE ALARM WOKE SAM IN DARKNESS. SHE WENT to the living room, found her sister sleeping, and shook her shoulder. "Wake up," she said. Elena groaned.

Sam scrambled three eggs for their breakfast, left half on the table, and went to her room to finish dressing. She came out and turned on the living room light. The whole front of the house was lit bright now. Elena covered her head with her blanket. "Get up," Sam said. "You have to drive me."

"Drive yourself."

"No. You have to take the car today."

"No," Elena said. Her face was still covered. "What time is it?"

Sam checked her phone. Three fifty-six. "Already four. You need to come on." She could put Elena, squinty and pajamaed, into the passenger seat for the ride to the harbor—that'd be no problem—but they had to leave.

Elena brought the blanket down. "You go."

"You can't—"

"Go. I'll find a ride with someone else today, okay?"

"With who?"

"Kristine."

The other server at the club. Kristine was forever acting as though she and Elena were best friends. Sam didn't like her, the stupid texts she sent, her attempts at inside jokes.

"Okay?" Elena's eyes were shut.

Sam hesitated. Logistically, it made sense. "You're going to get a ride with her. You're not walking."

"Got it."

"Can you text me when—"

"Sam," Elena said. "I'm good. Please turn off the light when you leave, thank you."

So Sam walked out alone. Above her, the sky was black, scattered with endless stars, glittering. The moon was already below the horizon. She would see the sun rise from the galley, after her shift started, as the night lifted gradually to show powdery blue dawn. For now, though, the darkness held.

Seeing the stars spread out reminded Sam of being a little girl. She and Elena used to have summer sleepovers outside; they used to walk these woods together; they used to point skyward, tell stories, make up the names of different constellations. The Little Hare was one, she remembered. The Bearded Dwarf. But she couldn't remember which stars corresponded to which patterns they'd drawn. Really, they must have pointed to a different bunch of dots every time.

The air was cool and damp. The trees rustled. She started the car. Somewhere nearby, she imagined, a creature stirred.

S AM'S NEXT DAY OFF WAS SPENT TAKING HER MOTHER TO the medical center in Friday Harbor. Her mother wanted to sit every time in the doctor's office alone, but it was Sam's responsibility to drive her to and from, to wait through the length of the appointment. Sam spent those hours walking in town from shop to shop. She held her cellphone in one hand. The receptionist at the clinic always called eventually to tell her to bring the car around.

It was a Tuesday morning, warm and clear. Getting into June at last. In two weeks, the ferry would switch to its summer schedule, and Sam was preparing for busy boat-loads of people, tourists crammed in front of her register and out on the decks. Before the pandemic, she sometimes worked doubles on summer weekends, which meant time and a half. Enough money to save. Elena kept the papers that tracked their finances piled on the kitchen table; Sam wanted to make enough in this peak season to see that stack decrease.

But today Sam wasn't working. Over these brutal past couple years, she'd become her mother's chauffeur, and even now, after her shifts had started again on the ferry, she needed to coordinate her schedule with her mother's doctor appointments. Elena's regular hours had supported them through their tightest times, as the boats stopped sailing, the tourists stopped coming, and the virus spread. They couldn't disrupt Elena's work—they depended on it. Sam had to be the one to handle anything that came up during the day at home. So someone else was getting paid to be on concessions this morning. Sam was wandering for free through town.

She ought to be doing surveys, making her time count, but she couldn't concentrate. Instead she spent a while looking at the art, carved wooden fish and ocean watercolors, in the window of Pearl Studios. Her reflection was sharp in the glass.

During the drive that morning, her mother had asked for details about Elena and the bear. "She saw it again?" her mother said. Sam didn't know how their mother had gotten this information—her bedroom was a place that seemed insulated from the rest of the house. The television played at all hours in there, keeping out other noise. The oxygen tank blasted away. Their mother, fatigued, napped much of the day, and called out at night, and kept her own hours. She had taken them through childhood; now she needed them to take her the rest of the way.

"What, Elena told you that?" Sam asked.

"I heard you two talking about it."

Sam kept her eyes on the road. Yes, she told their mother, Elena had, but then Sam massaged the story to ease its telling: they'd been farther from each other and moved on more quickly. The sighting became an instant, a blip. Two beings squinting at one another from opposite shores.

Still, the details Sam did give surprised their mother. Worried her. "Right there on the trail?" she asked. The long fence surrounding the airport streamed by their car windows. In the passenger seat, their mother was quiet, thinking, almost certainly, about her older daughter's brush with destruction. She looked worn out. Too thin. Her lips were cyanotic, touched blue.

When Sam and Elena were little, their mother was stunning to them. Even recalling that time, Sam could not see her as anything else. To a stranger's eyes, maybe she had been just some young woman who flat-ironed her hair for dates and wore low-rise jeans that were tight around her thighs, a woman who was poor and stuck and aspiring, who wore brown lipstick in the style of the times but was really no different from Sam and Elena today. Yet Sam thought of her as a goddess. Their mother was so lovely back then. That sleek hair, those mascaraed lashes, that tiny waist.

Her smile. Sam, who in seventh grade had been caught shoplifting bleach strips from the drugstore, and who'd stared after the symmetrical mouths of movie stars on tabloid covers and the orthodontics worn by girls at school, longed for a smile like that. Their mother's top six front teeth were straight and white and dazzling—perfect— courtesy of a bridge after a series of extractions in her teens. "You don't want these," their mother said, tapping on her false teeth. But Sam did. Their mother explained it—the bad appointments with a mainland dentist, promises made and teeth pulled and money handed over to fix nothing. "That guy didn't know what he was doing," their mother said, "and neither did I." Except their mother had a way of making even mistakes look gorgeous. She turned dentist visits and long labors and two kids and chest pain into the glamorous world of adulthood.

Their mother had been young. Impossibly young. By the time she was Sam's age, her children were already in first grade and kindergarten. Sometimes she would surprise them at school pickup, and the other kids would whisper about how pretty she was. Sam and Elena were delighted to go with her. They would've followed her anywhere. At home, when she laughed, she tilted her head back far enough that they could see where her bridge ended and her real teeth began, those secret dark spots at the back of her mouth. She was the woman they wanted to grow up to be.

Elena's plan had made them into that, in a way. And Sam had agreed. They'd done it together: stepped into their mother's shoes, in their mother's house. Their mother, in her turn, moved into the bedroom that their grandmother had occupied. They were playing the roles set out for them generations earlier.

In the car, her mother said, "Do you think it's safe for her to walk to work and back?"

"She's getting rides," Sam said. "With Kristine."

Her mother exhaled at that. "Growing up," she said, "we used to have so many foxes by the house. Did you know that? Mimi would leave out treats for them. They were adorable. Sweet as cats."

It was good to watch her mother's mood lift. "Are cats sweet?" Sam asked.

Her mother laughed. "Sweet ones are." Her shoulders, beneath the strap of the seatbelt, looked so fragile as to be breakable.

Was Elena actually getting a ride every day? She certainly said she was. Sam had seen her come home on foot on Sunday evening, though; when Sam questioned her, Elena said Kristine had been dropping her off at the corner.

Elena said, too, that she'd called the sheriff after her sighting in the woods, but Sam had looked on the *Journal*'s website for what details Elena would've had to provide and found nothing. Maybe the sheriff's office didn't share information with the newspaper. Or maybe reporters were tired of the same old bear-spotting stories. Maybe, probably, everyone else was ignoring what Elena said.

After their brush with Social Services in high school, Elena had accepted, immediately, that authority couldn't be trusted. The fact hadn't seemed to disturb her. She simply adjusted her behavior—no time spent after class with teachers, no visits with the guidance counselor, no unhappy truths revealed to social workers or well-meaning neighbors or even their own mother—and moved on. But Sam, in the years since, had trouble sticking to her sister's good example. Some naïve piece of Sam still wanted an authority to take care of things. A police officer or a school principal, a boss, a leader. Sam wanted a grown-up to step in, so she could step back and be a child again.

Well, no one was going to do that. Sam and Elena were the grown-ups now. With her mother dropped off, Sam was free to gaze through the glass of Pearl Studios, lose herself in the blue brushed landscapes, and let her worries about her sister go. Elena knew what she was doing: she'd contacted whomever she needed to contact; she had her commute under control. There was nothing in the newspaper because the bear, and everyone around them, had moved on.

And now that it was gone, and she was safe, Sam let herself, deliciously, enjoy it. There, standing on the sidewalk, as early-summer tourists brushed past, she remembered: she and her sister had seen a brown bear. At their front door! And it had thrilled Elena, made her voice hiccup and rise. Sam didn't want to forget that happy sound. The bear had done that for them, with its wet dark nose, its long snout, all its hair drawing back from its face as if combed. It delighted them. Let them laugh together. Its yellow eyes set into black-streaked fur, glowing there, lighting its watch.

The bear had brought them to the edge of disaster, then

left them in peace—what a gift. Massive and inconceivable, its presence. That dreadful, holy sight.

Cars rolled and slowed and turned on the street behind Sam's back. In the gallery windows, she stared through her own reflection, phone in hand.

The phone rang. She picked it up.

On the other end, a woman said, "Hi, Samantha?"

"Yes," Sam said. "She's ready?" The caller paused. Sam prompted her: "Michelle Arthur?"

"I may have the wrong number," the woman said. "I'm trying to reach Samantha Arthur."

Sam winced. "Who is this?"

"My name is Madeline Pettit. I'm calling from the Washington Department of Fish and Wildlife. This is Samantha?"

"Oh," Sam said. "Okay. Hi. Yes." She'd thought it was a debt collector—had been kicking herself for answering instead of letting it ring through. Elena always told her not to pick up unknown numbers. Sam had just been drifting, waiting for the medical center to call.

"I understand you had quite the encounter the other day."

"My sister did. Yes."

A keyboard clicked. "On June second at your home. On Portland Fair Road? That was your sister?"

"Oops," Sam said—the first one, the woman was talking about the first one—"Right, yes, no, we were both there. We both saw it. At the house."

"I see. Well, I'm calling to follow up. Is now a good time to talk?"

Sam turned away from the gallery. A line was forming at the ice cream stand next door. "Yeah."

"I'm sure you're busy," Madeline Pettit said. "I'll keep it brief. It's not unprecedented for black bears to come through the San Juans. We've had two in the last five years."

"Right. The police told us."

"Not unprecedented," Madeline said, "but unusual."

"Special," Sam said.

The tiniest pause. Then: "Rare. Certainly. So when there is a visit, we want to understand what, exactly, it consists of. We want to make sure everything's all right."

"Okay." Sam was ready to answer. The bear's face, its hair and its eyes, was fresh.

"The report I have here says it approached your door. I'm assuming there are some attractants on your property. Do you keep bird seed outside? Pet food? A grill?"

"No," Sam said. Kids stepped out from behind the ice cream stand's line. They weren't from here; the way they looked made it obvious. Their fists were coated in sprinkles.

"How secure are your garbage cans?"

Sam didn't know how to measure that. She guessed: "Pretty secure."

Madeline didn't believe her. Sam could tell by her voice. Madeline went on, tone firm—"The issue is that once a bear's found food around one home, it'll go, in the future, to other homes in the hope of finding more. That behavior endangers the bear's life. We therefore ask Washingtonians to store their garbage inside sturdy enclosures. Never leave it outside overnight."

"We don't. It didn't touch any of our garbage."

"Do you keep chickens? A chicken coop can be a feast of calories."

"It just sat there. That's all."

The keyboard clicked again. "That's great," Madeline said. "Please do continue to do your part to keep our bears wild. It's mating season, so they're on the move. Usually, they show up in a few backyards, turn over a garbage can or two, then pass out of an area relatively quickly."

Sam said, "This one was hanging around."

When Madeline spoke next, her voice was sharper. She was awake. "Was it?"

"Yeah."

"How so?"

"I guess . . ." Sam, childish, wanted Madeline to have a second report in front of her. Elena's call from the Friday before. The second approach.

"Do you mean that it was at your home for a long time that day, or that you saw it again after?"

Across the street, Danny Larsen's mother, getting out of her car, saw Sam, gave a wide smile, and waved. Sam waved back and turned toward the gallery. She preferred the privacy: her face toward the glass. She doubted whether

Elena would approve of what she was saying, so this position was better, a place where secrets might be kept. "Saw it again," she said.

"When and where?"

"On the trail," Sam said, "on Cattle Point Road, on Friday . . . around five-thirty . . ."

The typing noise had started again and wasn't letting up. "Five-thirty in the morning or evening?"

"Evening."

"And what did you see?"

Sam had to stop, then. She could see herself in the window—her posture. Her phone was pressed to her ear, her head was lowered, and her shoulders curved in, making a shelter around this call, trying to keep the knowledge of her betrayal out. Elena wouldn't like this. Wouldn't do this. Sam was doing something she knew was wrong.

So she tried to back up. "I actually didn't see anything."

"Uh-huh. You said before, your sister did?"

"She"—Sam stumbled over herself—"Yes." How had the woman guessed that? Sam couldn't remember—she'd told her already? What had Sam said?

Madeline's typing barely hitched. "This would be Michelle?"

"No. Elena," Sam said. Trying to think back to the beginning of their conversation. Distracted, she added, "Michelle's our mom."

"Ah. I have her here in the original report." Madeline read out Elena's cellphone number. "Is that right?"

"Right."

"Same residence?" Sam confirmed it. "Then tell me. To the best of your understanding. What exactly happened the second time around?"

The discomfort that had been rising and falling in Sam since she'd picked up this call—the anxiety and guilt, the flush of relief, the readiness followed by surliness, the suspicions and suggestions and doubts—and under those, all of them, the desire to find out exactly what had happened from this scientist's view, the nature of the visitation they'd received—that discomfort peaked. Sam felt like shit, to be precise. She was demanding the attention, yet again, of a stranger with power. Someone who could punish or fine or hurt them. The sort of person Elena said would never act to help.

Why couldn't Sam just practice accepting, like Elena did, what came to them each day? The long list of obligations. Sam complained about those, but Elena didn't; Elena went back and forth to work, quietly managed their finances, and shrugged. Or the short, shocking visions of beauty—the bear—Elena confided in no one but Sam, Elena kept their household confidences. While Sam could not. Sam told everyone, from the deckhands to random government bureaucrats. She had fantasized about alerting the newspaper. She couldn't seem to satisfy herself, even temporarily, with their lot.

One day, they would leave San Juan. Their world would expand, grow richer and more stable. The happinesses would come constantly, and the rest would drop away, but Sam would never make it to that point with her sanity intact if she didn't start trying, right now, to match the equanimity of her sister. They had a plan. They were going to get out of here. Beyond that, nothing mattered. Everything else, the tedious and the glorious, could be borne.

Sam had gotten this far into this call by being desperate, practically begging for intervention. But they didn't need it. Didn't want it. These lives would soon be behind them. She had to channel Elena, the clearest, calmest person she knew.

"Not much," Sam said.

Madeline waited for her to continue. When Sam didn't, Madeline prompted, "She saw the bear."

"Right." The line was silent. Sam said, "That's all."

"I'm interested in the details," said Madeline. "Was it eating? Was it moving? How close was it?"

"I don't know." Sam had already told Madeline too much. The rest was theirs.

Madeline sighed. "That's fine. Thank you. I'll reach out to her to ask."

A middle-aged couple brushed by Sam on their way into the gallery. Sam recognized them from the ferry: hot chocolate, black tea, complaining because the milk tasted sour. The husband had told her she didn't know how to do her job. They didn't recognize her.

Madeline said, "I'll be on the island tomorrow to meet

with the sheriff's office about the situation. Is there a good time after eleven for me to visit your home?"

"I'm not sure about that," Sam said. "You should coordinate with Elena."

Madeline pressed on. "Will you be home then? I'd like to assess the property."

"Talk to Elena," Sam said. "You have her number or whatever. But I'm afraid I'm expecting a call so I have to jump off the phone."

And the medical center was calling, then. It was an excuse, but it was the truth, too, Sam's mother required her. Madeline was asking something else but Sam had to go. She ended their call without mentioning that Elena was at work now and wouldn't pick up the phone from this number anyway and would never respond to a government office's voicemail. The fish and wildlife team could go on a bear hunt without them.

"Your mom is ready for you," the receptionist said. "And please do come into the office when you get here. We would like to have a word."

THEIR MOTHER WAS DYING. SAM AND ELENA AND THEIR mother herself knew it. The doctor knew it, and knew that they knew, so shared his assessment after her appointment without any hesitation or tenderness: her condition had worsened. Her pulmonary arteries showed more damage than at her last visit, and her right ventricle, pushing harder to pump blood through damaged vessels, had further enlarged. Her heart was straining. Eventually its muscle would weaken enough to fail. When Sam asked how long *eventually* might be, he said he didn't know. Eventually, he repeated. She would pass by heart failure, or, perhaps, a blood clot, or a sudden gush of blood into the lungs. His message to Sam, a reiteration, was that at some point, from one cause or another, she would go.

Her mother sat in a vinyl-wrapped chair in his office while he recited this. Sam, from the other chair, reached for her hand. Her mother squeezed back. Her slim fingers wrapped around Sam's palm. Her fingernails were pale and smooth as the sliced almonds in the salads served at the golf club; her pulse was fast, alarming, the rhythm of a bird's chest clenched in Sam's fist.

The doctor showed them to the reception desk, where, he said, they needed to discuss their account. There, a woman showed Sam numbers she didn't understand. The woman spoke firmly. Her surgical mask creased with every movement of her mouth. Sam's mother leaned against the counter. At one point, she shut her eyes, and Sam said, "I need to get my mom home."

Her mother opened them again. "I'm sorry. Just tired."

"Nothing to be sorry for," Sam said. She took the notices from the woman at the front desk, then helped her mother out the door. After she led her mother to the car at the curb, she texted Elena: *Appt done, heart not great. Let's discuss newest info together*

Their mother's death was on its way. This wasn't a surprise. Still, Sam was shaken. She gripped the steering wheel and guided the car through the town's roundabouts. Her mother, in the passenger seat, looked at the low houses passing by. Above the noise of the engine, Sam could hear her mother's breathing. Thin and rapid. As it always was. How much longer would Sam get to hear that sound?

The phone vibrated in Sam's lap when they were already out of Friday Harbor. She glanced down to read it. *Ok thanks. New info over here to talk about too*

"Is that Elena?" their mother asked.

Sam pressed a button on the phone to darken the screen. "Yeah."

"Is she home?"

"She should be," Sam said. The grill had closed an hour earlier.

Her mother said, "Don't worry, baby." Sam glanced over at her, then back at the road. She wanted to cry when she looked at her mom. When Sam was little, if she was frightened, she would press her face against her mother's thighs, and her mother would bend to rub circles on Sam's back, and whisper in Sam's ear: it's all right. You're all right. Sam wanted that, exactly that. The warm pressure of her mother's hand between her shoulder blades. It's all right.

But it wasn't. And there was nothing to cry about in that fact. This was how it was.

"I'm not worried," Sam said.

"Good."

They kept driving. On the side of the road, cows stared, dumb-eyed and helpless, over an unending fence. At a stop sign, Sam said, "I just want you to be comfortable."

"I am," her mother said. "I'm fine."

"I don't want you to be in pain."

Her mother sighed. The constricted sound of that air— it hurt Sam to listen. "You know what, Sammy, does it help you to hear that I'm used to it?"

The car's blinker was on. Sam said, "I guess."

Her mother was looking out the passenger-side window. "When your grandmother passed," she said, "I was

with her. She'd spent her last week kind of . . . in and out.
She wasn't totally conscious. I took those days off work. I
didn't know when it would be. Every time I made a meal
for you girls, or went to the bathroom, or had to change a
diaper, I was scared that she would go without me, but she
held on."

Sam didn't know what kind of response her mother
wanted. She guessed: "That sounds so hard."

"It was beautiful," her mother said. "She waited for me.
In the end, we were together—it was at night, I was in her
room—and her breath changed. It sounded different. It got
slow. I held her hand through it. I told her how much I
loved her—how much I'd always loved her, all my life. It
would go quiet, and I'd think that there it was, that had to
have been her last breath, but then she would breathe again.
It went on like that for hours, until there was no breath
anymore."

They were parked at the house by now. The trees leaned
over them. The engine was running. Sam turned the key to
shut it off.

Her mother said, "I'm so grateful I got to be with her in
that moment. To help her go."

The trees grew thick, branches laced together. Sam
stared out the windshield at their shapes. Inside the car, the
air was cool, and her mother, Sam felt, was waiting for
something, but Sam didn't know what that something was.

"I wish I remembered her," Sam said.

"She adored you two."

Sam and Elena were toddlers when their grandmother died. Their mother had practically been a child herself—three years younger than Sam was now—but she had already, at that age, done so much. Brought two people into life. Accompanied another person out of it.

The spectacular young woman their mother used to be. Before her boyfriend moved in, before sickness, back when the sisters were small. Their gorgeous girlish mother: cropped shirts, false teeth, impeccable pedicures. Lying on the floor between their beds in the dark to whisper assurances to Sam after nightmares. Coming home with her cash tips and giving Elena, with a flourish, a ten-dollar bill. Acting like they were rich. Like she was doing wonderfully. And the sisters, in their innocence, believing her. Revering her. The way their mother had taken care of them, until she couldn't anymore.

Carefully, Sam said, "Is there something you need from us? Or want? That kind of . . . the way you helped Mimi?"

"Oh, my baby," her mother said. "Thank you. No. I'm glad we're together, that's all."

"We're not going anywhere." Sam said it so easily. Because it was what her mother needed to hear, but also because it was true, they weren't going anywhere, were they, not while their mother was alive. Except the arc of those words out of her own mouth was like a nail sunk into Sam's chest. She had said it without thinking: her biggest fear. That idea was more horrible than a bear's tooth, more vivid than a death rattle. It punctured her.

"Well, good." Her mother's voice was light.

"Good," Sam said. "Great." The day's errand was over at last.

Getting out of the car, Sam slammed the driver-side door, making a sound that carried into the woods. This late in the day, their property was long with shadows. It was quiet and brown and green. Somewhere out there, beyond the hills and houses, the sound of the car door's slam was still traveling. It was passing over the edge of the island and along the ripples of the sea.

The air smelled like it had the other day. Like fresh shit.

Sam went to help her mother out of the passenger seat. Her mother straightened, gripping Sam's shoulder, and wrinkled her nose. "Ugh."

"Let's get inside," Sam said.

The front door of their house opened and Elena stepped out. She had showered, changed from her uniform, knotted her hair into a bun. It wasn't yet that magical hour before sunset, the time of day when the sky turned pink and honey, but Elena glowed.

"Do you want help?" Elena asked.

Sam said, "We got it."

"Come get my bag?" their mother asked. Elena came over to take the purse from the car. Her mouth was tipped up at the corners, a tiny smile. She was somewhere Sam was not. Their mother added, "Do you smell that?"

Elena raised her head. Her thin neck stretched.

That stink: meat, fur, oil, earth. There was no second

pile on their sidewalk, but the weight of it, the taste, hung in the air. An animal had left its scent there. Sam didn't want her family to be outside anymore.

In the kitchen, Elena made a fried egg over black beans for their mother, who ate a bite before pausing to catch her breath. Sam told Elena about the new receptionist at the medical center who had blue hair. And a crystal stud, their mother added, set into the skin right here—she touched the top of her cheekbone. How had Sam not noticed that? "That's called a dermal piercing," Elena said, leaning over to borrow their mother's fork, share a bit of the beans. Their mother pushed the plate toward her and Elena pushed it back. "How do you know that?" Sam asked. Elena shrugged. She encouraged their mother to eat a little more. Their mother tried.

Head propped on her hand, Sam watched them. Elena was making some joke; their mother chuckled. It had been Sam's day off, yet her sister, who'd just worked a full shift, was the one who looked refreshed. She was luminous. Her eyes shone. The idea entered Sam's mind of their grandmother lying in the dark—the sounds she must've made, gasping toward death. Would they hear their mother's breath change that same way? But Sam pushed that image out. She didn't want to think about it. Elena was telling a story about a customer.

Dusk had fallen by the time their mother headed to bed. Sam wiped grease from the stove. Down the hall, she could hear Elena's voice, their mother's low responses. The toilet flushing, the water running, a door opening and shutting again. The rush of the oxygen tank. Elena's footsteps coming back.

Entering the kitchen, Elena said, "So how was it really?"

"Bad," Sam said. "The ventricle looks worse."

"What's her PAP?"

"I don't remember the exact number. They gave me a printout." Elena went to the hall to dig into Sam's jacket pockets. Sam went on: "Fifty, maybe?"

Elena returned, papers in hand. Her forehead creased as she skimmed them. "Sammy."

"What?"

"A hundred twenty." Elena sat at the table. She was pinching the papers. Her skin was tight over her jaw. "That's really bad."

Sam said, "You don't need to tell me that. I know."

"You should've told me right away."

"I—" What was the difference, to have texted her from the office or showed her now? What did it change? But then—Sam looked again at Elena's face, the tension there. Elena had to take on the role of caring for them; the least Sam could do was give her what she needed to do that job.

Elena turned a page over and shook her head. She set that sheet aside on the table. It was what the woman at the reception desk had tried to discuss with Sam when they were leaving: their account, the amount owed. Sam said, "They're mad about that."

"I'm on it," Elena said. "Don't worry."

"The lady said we're overdue or whatever."

Elena put the papers down and pressed her fingers to her brow bone. Her nails were shaped like their mother's, thin ovals, but flushed with more color. Her hands hid her eyes for a moment. Then she lowered them, revealing herself again. "I'm handling it. Okay?"

Sam took a chair. On the table between them, Elena's phone vibrated, and Elena turned it over, checked the screen, put it down. Sam twisted her mouth: "Kristine?" Elena mm-hmmed. "What's she saying?"

"Nothing important," Elena said. She picked the papers back up. "Tell me about the rest of the day."

Sam blew her breath out. Every appointment she drove her mother to was made up of tiny unremarkable griefs: the doctor's tone, their mother's posture. She owed Elena the details but they were too dull to share.

Instead, then, of talking about Dr. Boyce's repeated concerns, Sam said, "During the ride, she talked about Mimi dying."

"Oh, yeah?"

"She said it was beautiful to be with her. That's the word she used." Elena pressed her lips together. Sam said, "She said she was glad we're here with her now."

The house around them was quiet. Down the hall, from behind their mother's door, came the faint noise of televised voices, but that was a background hum. It was nothing more intrusive than the refrigerator running or the faint whistle, outside, of the wind. "Well," Elena said, letting her voice drop into the stillness. "We're all glamorous beauties here."

The papers were set aside. Sam and Elena sat together in silence. There was so much that didn't need to be spoken. How long they'd been in this exact position, standing at their mother's death's door—waiting for the latch to give, and for their mother to pass through at last.

When they first learned her diagnosis, the sisters had cried over it together. Sam felt shattered. That was back when she pictured pain as something swift and final. She understood better, now, what it actually was—not a glass dropped onto a tile floor, one terrible burst, but a tree required to grow over years in a space that limited it. Branches curled in on themselves, leaves dropping. A living thing that was forced, relentlessly, to submit.

That was how sorrow acted on them. Sam wanted more for her mother, but the wanting was useless, the wanting didn't change anything. Their mother was dying, whether they wanted it or not. Most of the treatments the doctors recommended to improve her quality of life—not to actually fix her lungs, they emphasized, but to make her feel better, for a while—weren't covered under their insurance, so she would suffer on her way to the end. She had been suffering for a long time. At some point, she would be in enough distress that Sam or Elena would have to stay with her, constantly, to manage the equipment, the tank and the mask, and if that point came during peak season, their household might have to forfeit half its yearly income. And then the bills would come. Sam knew their mother's death was near—it couldn't be avoided—and when she thought of it, some part of her, the waiting part, the grieving part, the part that had doubled back on itself with pain, did wish to be past it already. If Sam's heart broke from the loss, then it broke; what difference did having a whole heart make anyhow? Let it be destroyed. She just needed the long ache to stop.

Elena leaned over, her chest pressed to the table, and whispered, "Sorry, but I have to tell you something."

"Okay," Sam said.

"Except you can't tell Mom."

Sam shook her head. "I won't."

Elena was indeed a beauty. Her hair, swept up on top of her head, pulled her forehead tight, made her brows rise. Her eyes were wide. Their blue was pale, luminous, holes made in ice. Sam leaned forward, too—she couldn't help herself. Elena said, "The bear came back."

THERE, AT THE TABLE, ELENA EXPLAINED. SHE HAD gotten home from work and gone to shower. Under the rush of the water, she'd heard, from outside, a thump. Then another. It sounded like something hitting against the front wall, Elena said. Like a branch falling. Something solid.

As Elena stepped out, in her towel, she kept listening, and it happened again, that sound of contact. She went into the living room and saw, through the front window, the enormous furred body of an animal. A brown bear moving against the house.

Sam was full of dread. "Moving how?"

"He had his back against the corner"—Elena straightened in her seat, pulled her shoulders back—"And was rubbing against it. He would go like—" She wiggled side to side, shaking her head in the air, imitating. "Back and forth, up and down. Making a rhythm."

"What the hell," Sam said. She couldn't think of anything else cogent. Elena's miming put Sam in mind of a million competing foolish images: a cartoon creature in a

Disney movie scratching itself on a tree, a snake moving across sand, a dog humping a leg, two pieces of wood rubbed together to make fire.

"It was wild," Elena said. "I was at the window and he was right there, maybe—ten feet away? Just on the other side of the glass."

Sam didn't understand how her sister had moved toward the window. She wanted to go look at the living room, to retrace Elena's steps into that corner in order to make the walk seem somehow reasonable, but she was scared to move that way, scared even to stand. The bear had been at the house less than an hour before. It might still be on their property, watching. "You were right at the window?" she asked.

Elena nodded with—was that delight?

Elena's elation was more than confusing. It was distressing. It made Sam doubt her sister's judgment, which she never had before. This glow on Elena's face. This smile. Sam said, "Why?"

The muscles around Elena's eyes contracted. A wince or a squint. "Why?"

"Weren't you terrified?"

"Oh my god. Of course I was," Elena said. And the relief—Sam was rocked by it—of course Elena was terrified. Elena knew how dangerous this was, an animal pressed to the side of their home. Elena was amazed by its novelty, yes, but she wasn't kept by that amazement from the truth.

Sam's palms were slick from minute-old sweat. She wiped them against her thighs. This was supposed to be her day off, but instead she'd been worn down for hours by routines, old pains, and then surprises and new adrenaline, and she was exhausted by it all, her body was collapsing. Her brain wasn't working anymore. "I don't understand why it keeps coming here."

"He's only come a couple times."

"That's a lot. Is it not a lot?" Sam didn't mention the shit outside, the scratches.

"No," Elena said, "it is. You're right." She paused. "I don't know."

"If we had . . . a bird feeder or something out there for it to eat, I'd understand, but . . ."

"I mean, we don't know what attracts him," Elena said. "We're not bear experts."

"Did you talk to that woman today?"

Elena frowned at her. "What woman?"

"The bear expert." Elena looked blank, and Sam said, "She called maybe around three? And was going to call you?"

"Who is this?"

"Sorry," Sam said. She wasn't yet thinking straight. A pane of glass separating them from the creature was not enough. Its presence outside made being in this house, which Sam knew so well as a plain, steady thing, seem unpredictable. She shut her eyes, took a breath, started over:

"One of the state wildlife people called. She was asking questions about the bear and she wanted to set up a time to stop by. I told her to talk to you."

Elena was scrolling on her phone. "Oh, yeah," she said. "I see."

"You didn't talk to her?"

"I was at work."

"I know," Sam said. "Sorry. Just freaking out."

Elena put the phone down. Reached to take one of Sam's hands, pull it over the table, cup it. "Don't. We're okay."

"But why is it coming here?"

Elena's fingers were cool and dry and strong. Her eyebrows, dark blond lines, were knit, and Sam could see at once the girl she'd been, the kid who'd led them through the forest, and the older woman she would grow to be. Elena repeated, "We're okay."

They sat like that. The house settled around them. Water through pipes, wind against walls, the little shifts of a building standing though it was not built to last. Elena held Sam. They listened.

"You're worried about Mom," Elena said.

"I guess."

"You are." Elena squeezed. "I get it."

The television in the back of the house had shut off sometime during their conversation. Their mother must be sleeping by now. Sam said, "We've been waiting so long for things to get better."

"I know."

"And they keep getting worse and worse."

"We're going to get through this," Elena said. "We always do." Her voice was firm. She released Sam's hand. "Want tea?"

When Sam nodded, Elena went to the cupboard to get out the bags of powdery chamomile. She filled two mugs with tap water and put them in the microwave. Her back was to the table. From behind, in her after-work clothes and her high bun, she looked like she was eighteen again, standing at their kitchen counter to wait for the beep that meant dinner was ready. In moments like this, Sam could almost let the last eleven years go.

"Thanks," Sam said when Elena brought over her steaming mug.

Elena returned to the microwave to fetch her own. Over her shoulder, she said, "Some things are getting better already."

"Yeah?"

"Yeah." She came back to the table with two spoons and a container of honey.

Sam wasn't sure. "Like what?"

Elena shrugged. Gestured toward the living room, the corner of the house rubbed by a bear, the night outside. The world. And Sam imagined, then, what might be coming: a raise for Elena at the club; a reliable schedule for Sam made up of only afternoon shifts; a prospective buyer reaching out about the property. There were, she supposed, always chances for hope. She took her mug by its handle and smiled at her sister.

Elena smiled back. "I promise," she said. "You'll see."

They sipped their teas. The drink was too hot in Sam's mouth, but she drew it in anyway, let it go down. Her fingertips burned on the sides of the mug. Her sister, across the table, was still smiling, a little. Lips closed in a curve over her overlapping canine. The corners of her eyes were crinkled. She was happy.

When they were girls, after school let out, Sam and Elena used to wander the single mile down to Jackson Beach. They'd climb over log after log, each as high as their shins and as white as a bone, to the line where the shore met the water. In that place, they'd find tide pools. Bright green anemones, miniature crabs, sucker fish hidden under stones.

They had never had enough money, Sam knew, and had never really had any friends, and eventually, under the pressure of their mother's boyfriend, had been treated badly, used, but the two of them always found their own reasons to go on. They had the versions of paradise they made. Places that were tiny, salt-smelling, barely visible to anyone else. Places that were, and would be, their own.

Elena turned the honey over. "Do you think bears actually like this?"

"Let's not find out."

The container rotated in Elena's fingers. The honey

shifted, molten gold. Elena's face, regarding it, was lit soft yellow. The kitchen lights shone white overhead.

"Are you going to call that woman back?" Sam asked.

"Who?"

"The expert," Sam said. "From the state."

Elena put the honey down. "Let's see."

"She wanted to come by tomorrow."

"I'm working tomorrow."

"I know," Sam said. "But after my shift. I could meet her."

Elena stood to rinse her tea out in the sink. "I don't know what there is to meet about, anyway."

The grizzly bear pressing itself to our house, Sam wanted to scream—the threat of mauling. Instead she got up and handed Elena her empty mug. "Maybe give her a call," Sam said.

From her bedroom, after, Sam could hear the clanging of dishes, the nighttime noise of Elena washing up. Her phone showed three texts from Ben. Silly jokes and jabs. She didn't feel like reading them. Instead she lay on her back and tapped through a survey. It asked her how often she wore perfume: never, not often, sometimes, often, always. She picked always. It broke up the monotony to pretend she was living a different life. Then she navigated over to the website for the Washington Department of Fish and Wildlife and scanned their employee directory. There she was: Madeline Pettit. An email address.

Sam did trust Elena. Completely—with everything

from their finances to their future. She was only looking this up because she knew her sister, her history, her quirks, and so knew that Elena would never contact the state for help, and knew, beyond that, that at this moment they ought to.

So Sam sent an email. *Hi Madeline, my name is Sam Arthur. You called asking about coming to our house on Portland Fair Road on San Juan. I'll be home at 1pm tomorrow and can meet you then.* Elena wouldn't be home until six. That would give them the time to wrap everything up. *Looking forward,* Sam tapped out on the screen, and *Thanks.*

THE BIOLOGIST ARRIVED FIVE MINUTES EARLY THE NEXT afternoon. The doorbell rang while Sam was in her mother's bedroom setting up lunch. Her mother straightened in bed. "Who's that?"

"Ah," Sam said, putting the plate down on the bedside table. A tomato and mayonnaise sandwich. Her heart was racing from the chime. Having this meeting without Elena felt like an indiscretion, but it wasn't, it was normal, a minor chore. To emphasize that to herself, Sam said to her mother, "Someone's here about the bear."

Her mother's eyes were large. "What about it?"

"To check that nothing we have is attracting it."

"Are we in trouble?"

"No," Sam said, "no, no," but her pulse stayed fast. She turned up the volume of the TV. Refilled her mother's water, fixed a pillow behind her mother's back, then let herself out, closing the bedroom door after. The doorbell rang again. Sam pressed her lips shut.

She opened the front door to find a small, handsome

woman, with a strong jaw and beautiful teeth and dark hair brushed back from her forehead. Madeline Pettit said, "Samantha?"

"Sam."

"That's right." Madeline showed her identification: a tiny photo of her face, a green logo. "When you didn't answer, I thought you might not be here after all."

"Sorry. I'm here. I just had to deal with my mom first. She's sick." Madeline's eyebrows tipped up. This was how polite people showed how sorry they were. Sam said, "Do you want to come in?"

Madeline stepped over their threshold. She started unlacing her boots and Sam said, "You don't need to," and Madeline said, "Please, I've been in the dirt all day," and then straightened in her stocking feet. Her toes made tiny curves against the cloth. Madeline wore gray slacks and a tan button-down that had a state seal stitched over the breast pocket. Sam was in leggings and an old T-shirt. She was vividly embarrassed of her own body, the way it stood in clothes. She couldn't pinpoint Madeline's age, but Madeline did seem older. More together. Someone too busy to even remember Sam's nickname.

Sam said, "I actually work with the state, too."

Madeline had been looking down their hall, but she returned her attention to Sam. "Is that right?"

"I don't know if that was in the report you got. Yeah. Department of Transportation."

"No better benefits," Madeline said. Sam made herself smile. She had allowed Madeline to misunderstand, she knew—Sam worked, in fact, for Centerplate, the ferries' private food vendor—and so she didn't get any of the things that probably made a career at the Department of Fish and Wildlife, where employees played in the dirt all day, grand. But Sam worked somewhere, she did something, and Madeline ought to know that much, at least. Madeline asked, "What do you do there?"

"I'm on the ferries."

"How lovely. I came over from Anacortes this morning. It's a beautiful ride."

Sam looked again at Madeline's face, the sculpted shape of it. Had this woman stopped by the galley during Sam's shift? Ordered a croissant that Sam spent thirty seconds heating in the microwave? But wouldn't Sam have remembered her?

Madeline looked back at her blank. Not recognizing. She said, "So tell me what you saw."

Sam described the morning shock of the bear's first visit. Its enormous body at their door. She showed Madeline the pictures, the brown blur. Madeline, taking notes, asked questions: did Sam's family keep pets or livestock? Were there fruit trees on their property? Was there anything odorous in their cars? When Sam hesitated at the last one, Madeline rephrased. "Anything that smells."

"I know that," Sam said. "No."

"Our goal is keeping this bear from climbing what we call the behavioral ladder. Say it finds something appealing to eat in a garage. Then it goes into an empty house, does damage, makes the news. We tag it and relocate it, but a bear has a good memory, it comes back. Finally, it's unlucky enough to scare someone out in their yard. It's named a nuisance bear. It gets euthanized."

"Hold on. You're saying it could come into our house?" Sam asked.

"No." Madeline raised her note-taking hand, pen laced between fingers. "That level of behavior is up here." She slid her hand down in the air. "We're going to ensure this animal stays right here."

They both put their shoes on. They went outside, where Madeline squinted at the front step and took photos of the walkway. Sam studied the back of Madeline's head. The sleekness of her ponytail. Being in this position was oddly reminiscent of standing behind Elena when they were kids—waiting for Elena to rise from picking up shells and announce the rules of some fantastic game. It sent Sam back. After a few minutes, Sam said, "So that's what you do? Tag them and take them away?"

Without turning around, Madeline again raised one hand, marking an invisible rung on the imaginary ladder. "That's a response to escalated behavior," she said over her shoulder. "If the animal returns."

"But it has."

Madeline did turn then. "Is that so?"

"Yesterday," Sam said. "After we talked. It was right there."

Madeline followed the line of Sam's pointing to the corner of the house. She squatted there, in the dirt, then went slowly over the twenty feet between them. In the inspection, Sam saw Madeline's doubt—she saw judgment. Madeline seemed to think that there would be dog food, or ripe berries, or browning banana peels scattered across the ground. That Sam and her family were doing something wrong.

Madeline stopped at the section of damaged siding by the door. "Which incident is this from?"

"That's actually from before," Sam said. "Our neighbor said we might have voles."

Madeline reached out, slim-fingered, and touched the peeled vinyl edge of one strip of siding. She twisted it to look at both sides. "Quite the infestation." Turning her tan wrist, she displayed the loose piece. "See those? Teeth marks."

"Not a vole?" Sam asked.

"Not unless your voles weigh four hundred pounds."

Sam frowned.

Maybe in the high light of a June afternoon, Madeline couldn't see Sam's expression, because she continued talking, blithely. "Usually we see this on trees. They gnaw at them to get the sap flowing. Yours picked the wrong place to focus his attention—all he was going to get at here was insulation—but he tried his best. And smell that?"

Sam did, yes. Not as strong a stink as the day before, but still something. Musk and wet soil. Hair and skin.

"The bear's urinated here," Madeline said.

Sam stepped back. "Jesus."

Madeline smiled at Sam. In this sun, Madeline was perfectly illuminated. Her eyes shone. Brown-black, warm black, a rich velvety black that caught and cupped the daylight. Black that contained gold. Her cheeks were faintly, thoroughly freckled, a dust over her complexion. She looked like a woman who had everything. Every luxury, every opportunity. Sam could not even begin to imagine—what must it be like? Madeline said, "It'll fade."

Sam had to remember. "The smell."

"This bear has made your home into a kind of unnatural rub tree. They mark a trunk, or a place, more generally, in this instance, with their urine, the oil in their fur, their anal gland secretions—really, don't worry, it doesn't do any harm—in order to communicate."

"Communicate what?"

"Oh, well. Whatever it is they have to say. Their dominance, or that they're looking for a mate."

This was more alarming to Sam than Madeline, with her matter-of-fact tone, was giving room for. "Dominance?"

"It's mating season," Madeline said. "This is how animals talk to each other. They beat their chests and express their scent glands and generally show off how powerful they are."

"But why is it doing that here?"

"He's confused, I suppose."

Sam didn't like this. Any of it. The bear, its behavior, the source being confusion. The recurrence of the visits. Three times! Enough to make a biologist turn in surprise. And the marking. The bear had marked them. Sam asked, "So it's going to keep coming back?"

"No, no," Madeline said. "They have multiple rub spots. Think of it as a trail marker, not a destination."

"We're on a bear trail now?" said Sam, dread-filled. "So there'll be more?" Madeline shook her head. "But how do you know?"

"It's rare for one to come through these islands."

"But people say it's not. Another one came a couple years ago. And this one's here now."

Sam's voice was getting tighter, higher, but Madeline was refusing to match her. "Let me emphasize that it's extremely unusual," she said. She was selecting each word as though she was concerned that Sam, if pressed, might rush off like a panicked animal through the trees. "But at this time of year, males, especially, will travel long distances in search of potential mates. This one just happened, on his long trip, to cross paths with you. He's marking in order to signal his presence to females. He will keep moving, and keep marking, until he finds some."

"Except this one's not moving."

"Well," Madeline said, "he is. He came from the mainland to here. And soon, frustrated in his search, he'll leave."

Sam didn't know how to get through to her. Okay, yes,

the bear had come to them from elsewhere, it hadn't erupted entire from the ground in front of this door, but the point was that now it was here, over and over, not leaving. It was standing outside their entryway, rubbing itself on their windows, following Elena down isolated trails. Madeline had said this was rare, but it didn't matter to Sam, to her family, if usually, historically, such a thing didn't happen. It was happening. It was happening to them right now.

"I think you should remove it," Sam said. "I mean, I wouldn't have reached out if it wasn't serious. If taking it away is something you can do, then you should go ahead and do it."

Madeline sighed. "I hear you. That said, I don't see anything particularly alarming."

"Okay, but I'm alarmed," Sam said. Insisted. She could tell Madeline more, about Elena coming across the creature in the woods, but what was in front of them, on the wall and the ground, ought to be enough. "It has a habit of coming here. It's damaging the house, you told me, and that's a problem for us, we need to— We're going to be selling the house, we need it not to be hurt, we can't have it targeted by wild animals. My sister and I are counting on it. We're going to move soon."

Madeline showed no reaction to this, the revelation of Sam and Elena's greatest dream. The information submerged beneath her calm. She only said, "There's been no major harm done. I encourage you to reach out to your home insurance with your concerns. Depending on your level of coverage, they may pay for a repair."

Home insurance claims were the sorts of things Elena handled. As Sam watched, Madeline tucked her cellphone and notebook into her tote, which was embroidered, too, with the department's logo. Madeline's smooth beauty felt dissonant with the uniform; she didn't seem like the authorities Sam had known. But the next step from the state was clear: to abandon them. Madeline said, "Just don't approach him"—

"It's approaching us."

—"And all will be well. What you have here is an interesting, perhaps once in a lifetime, brush with nature. Keep a respectful distance and enjoy."

They finished things with each other out there in the yard. Madeline gave Sam a business card, and Sam kept trying to figure Madeline out. That elder-sibling attitude. Or was it simple arrogance? Like the thousands of other fancy people who rode across the channel each day? At the last goodbye, Sam couldn't help herself: "It's cool that you . . . how'd you wind up doing this?"

"I studied wildlife science in school. I've always been passionate about animals. How they behave, how we relate to them. My uncle used to take me trapping."

This polished woman setting traps among trees. "That's so funny," Sam said. "You don't look like you'd be good at this."

As soon as she heard herself, she knew it was wrong. Madeline's lips closed over her fine white teeth. No, Sam wanted to protest, I didn't mean—it was supposed to be—but no explanation would take the words back, and, god, how she hated it, the awkward child always spilling out of her, clumsy as ever, trying and failing to keep up as women like Madeline and Elena moved confidently ahead.

"If you need anything else, our office's contact information is on the card," Madeline said. "Do have a good day."

"You too," Sam said. Bitter. Embarrassed. A feeling she hated: embarrassment. A feeling she had to live with all the time.

Sam let herself into the house. She took off her shoes—they did have dirt on them, she supposed. Then she went to check on her mother. Helped her to the bathroom. Thought, while her mother sat on the toilet, about uniforms and ponytails, business cards, elegance. The end of her conversation with Madeline kept intruding. On her knees, Sam remembered her every error, the moments she'd made Madeline stop and squint and get crisp.

And then Sam refused those memories. She hadn't messed up, she assured herself. In fact the biologist had been the one acting strange. The toilet flushed, and through the noise Sam repeated that Madeline, not Sam, was wrong.

The rich, the overeducated, the people who believed themselves superior—those were the people Sam did not want to be around. Madeline wasn't like Elena. How dumb to have thought that. After her mother returned to bed, Sam headed to her own room. She brought up a new survey on her phone.

Outside, voices.

Elena. The rise and fall of Elena's voice through the wall—how? Now? Sam shoved her phone in her pocket and hurried to the door.

Elena was standing in her work clothes where their front walk met the road. Where Madeline's car was parked. Madeline was still there, talking to her. When Sam saw the two of them from the doorway, Elena glanced over, waved, pointed. "The bear expert!"

"What are you doing here?" Sam asked.

"A fuse blew in the kitchen," Elena said. "They sent us home until they fix it. They said it might be a few hours. And look who I found."

Sam's skin was hot. She was flushing, she knew. She went inside, pulled her shoes on, and exhaled, then came out to join.

"He could take down a small deer," Madeline was telling Elena when Sam got there. "But mostly roots, fruits, grains, insects."

"Fish," Elena suggested.

"Fish, sure. Small mammals. They're omnivores."

To Elena, Sam said, "Was she just telling you we don't need to worry about being attacked?"

Elena turned her gaze to Sam. In her black polo, with

her hair pulled back, Elena's face was dreamy, exhausted. She said, "We were talking about what bears eat," and Madeline, beside them, said, "My understanding was that you were mainly concerned about damage to the home. Are you worried about being attacked?"

Was Madeline making fun of her? She repeated Sam's words and made them sound idiotic, but they weren't. Anyone who had a bear prowling around their windows would worry about being attacked. Sam said, "Of course we are. There's a grizzly bear stalking us."

The other two dismissed that. "Come on," Elena said, and Madeline said, "He's not a grizzly." Elena faced Madeline with interest: "He's not?"

"No. I told your sister when we first spoke. He's a black bear, certainly."

"But he's not black," Elena said.

"Some can be cinnamon or even blond," Madeline said. The bear expert, monologuing again. "It's not the coloration that makes it a black bear. They're their own distinct species, more closely related to Asian black bears than North American browns."

"I'm so surprised," Elena said. "I think of black bears as smaller."

"They're medium-sized."

"This one's huge."

"Medium for a bear is still substantial," Madeline said. "Males are about five feet tall when standing upright. You wouldn't want to get in a tussle with one."

Low, Elena said, "He seems bigger than that."

Sam cut in, then, to support her sister. "Elena knows. It came right up to her the other day."

Madeline said, "Right. Well, seeing these animals up close, unexpectedly, can be shocking, and shock can do strange things to our perception." To Elena, she said, "I'm sure opening the door on one gave you quite a fright."

"It was all right," Elena said.

"No, it walked up to her outside, away from here," Sam said. "She saw it really well. She said it was a grizzly."

Madeline appraised them both. Then she reached into her tote to take out her notebook again. "This was the sighting you mentioned on the phone. Cattle Point Road."

"That's right," Sam said. "It came right up." Elena was looking at Sam. To her sister, then, Sam said, "Tell her."

Elena wasn't upset, her forehead was smooth, but she wasn't glad at this chance to talk, either. She wasn't anything. She was radically different from the way she'd been after that trail encounter: her million texts and calls, her rapid retellings, her shine. Sam found the change so irritating. This was how Elena had been in school, too, or behaved at the club when they worked together—to strangers, she was always friendly, smiling and making small talk, but flattened. She showed them none of her true self. Sam knew that Elena's excitement was there, trapped in her body, kept under high pressure by her skin, but Elena let it out for nobody but Sam, even in the moments, like this one, where it was required.

To Elena, Madeline said, "Right up to you? Really?"

"Not right up to me," Elena said. "A little bit away."

Sam had had enough of this. "You said thirty feet away."

"Maybe," Elena conceded.

"That must've been something," Madeline said.

Elena nodded. Smiled. Vague, patient. How many times had Sam stood beside her sister in public and watched this same fakery unfold? Where Elena gave nothing, agreed with everything, waited the moment out?

Madeline reviewed her notes. "This was Friday, June second? Your sister told me you saw the animal around five-thirty that evening?"

Elena said, "That sounds right."

"Are there any other details you can share?"

Elena, still pleasant, shook her head.

And Madeline closed her notebook. Sam couldn't understand why. Madeline was missing everything: the details of the bear's size, the bulk of its haunches, the light in its fur, the length of its claws. The enormous rippling energy that made Sam want to stare and scream at once. Its interest in Elena, its willingness to emerge. Its ears, its muzzle, its muscle. Everything that mattered, Madeline had missed.

"As I told Samantha, I don't see any cause for alarm," Madeline said. "Just be sure to keep your property free of attractants. Bear attacks really are very rare. When you saw him, was he standing on his hind legs?"

"Nope," Elena said.

"Well, if you do happen to see him again, and he is, re-member he's likely being inquisitive. They're curious ani-mals. As long as you don't attempt to feed or harm him, all will be well."

"So you're not going to do anything about it," Sam said. "Track it or trap it or—"

"We are tracking it," Madeline said, "to the extent pos-sible. That's why I came today." With her pen, her bag, her dismissals. "If he comes back, please call."

She was at last ready to leave. And Elena, clearly, was ready to go inside, but Sam, who had coordinated this day to resolve the matter of the bear and who had gotten from it no resolution at all, was truly frustrated. None of the bear behavior facts this woman had offered were going to keep Sam's home or her family safe. They couldn't wait around for this animal to step out from between the trees, rise to its hind legs, and snarl. Sam said, "What is calling you going to do for us?"

Elena put a hand on Sam's arm. Squeezed. Madeline said, "Are you thinking about a reward for capture?"

No. "Is there a reward?" Sam said.

Madeline frowned. "No."

Sam went hot with humiliation. With rage. Madeline had come to their house prepared to find trash, and she'd found it, hadn't she, money-hungry girls too naïve to know what they were talking about. Girls who didn't know what a brown bear was, or how high in the air five feet went, or where money came from or what it did. All day long, passengers spoke to Sam this same way: *I said no cream,* when they had said cream. Or asking what the best hiking path was on Shaw Island and rolling their eyes when she said they should look at a trail map. Their whole lives, Sam and Elena had been treated like fools. Forget it—forget reaching out for help from her. From anyone.

"WHAT A BITCH," SAM SAID, SITTING ON THE CLOSED toilet lid while Elena changed out of her work clothes in the bathroom. Elena took out her hair tie, combed her fingers through her hair, and gathered it again. She might've shrugged but her shoulders were raised already and Sam couldn't tell. "Didn't you think?"

"She seemed fine to me. Actually, I thought you were the one being kind of rude."

Sam leaned back in consternation. Her spine, with the movement, hit the tank, the cold hard ceramic knocking her vertebrae. "No."

Elena touched her hair one last time before putting her arms down. "Okay."

"You should've heard our conversation before you got there."

"If only," Elena said. She turned on the faucet to wash her face, but put just her fingers under, watching the flow, not taking the next step. Without looking at Sam, she said, "Why was she here?"

Since the moment Sam had heard Elena's voice outside,

she knew she would have to answer this question, and yet. How to make sense of it? Sam had done what she knew her sister would not want her to do. She opened her mouth to explain the choice that now seemed inexplicable. "I called her."

Elena bent forward, cupped the water, splashed her cheeks. Droplets spattered Sam.

"I know you have a lot on your mind. I figured I could take care of this one thing."

Elena's eyes were squeezed shut. She was rubbing soap into her cheeks. Her forehead was creased from the effort.

"I thought she would tell us how to get rid of it. She said it's been here more times than we thought—that it bit open the wall next to the front door. It's marked the house. I'm worried it's dangerous."

Elena straightened to face the mirror. Water beaded on her jaw and dripped off her chin. Sam passed her a towel from the rack. Elena said, "I hope you understand now that he isn't."

"That's what she said."

"You don't believe her?"

"I don't know."

Elena shrugged at her reflection. "Didn't you bring her here because you think she knows what she's talking about?"

Sam scoffed. She took the damp towel from Elena. Saw, as she hung it up, Madeline's lovely, undisturbed face, her small hands touching the side of their home. Sam's embarrassment surfaced once more, prickling on her skin. "She was so weird," Sam said. "Can't you picture her in freshman bio? Eager for a dissection or whatever."

Elena shook her head. Stripped of one layer of sweat and oil, her cheeks shone clean. "You're picturing all sorts of things these days." Before Sam could defend herself, Elena turned, rested her hip against the sink, and said, "Please don't bring her here again."

Sam shook her head back. A sister, an echo. "I won't."

"I don't appreciate your keeping secrets from me."

"It wasn't— I was trying to help."

Elena's washed face was clear and sharp and pale. The thin blond hairs at her hairline were darkened by water. There had been moments, over the past week, where Sam felt distant from her sister, kept at a remove from Elena's thrills, but here, now, Elena was entirely familiar. They were in this small room together and Elena was telling her what to do. Elena said, "What's going on here is not dangerous. It's magical. It's the best thing that has ever happened to us."

ELENA EXPLAINED: A CREATURE THAT DID NOT EXIST ON their island, did not belong in their lives, had nevertheless come. It swam long miles in the wet black night to arrive at their home. Made an exception of itself, and of them, to every rule. It was supposed to be gruff but was instead tender. It was supposed to be wild but behaved like it was tamed. It came to Elena on the path as gentle as a suitor. Is that not wonderful? she asked Sam. Doesn't that seem like magic to you?

"Is a raccoon getting into a garbage can magic?" Sam said. "It's an animal. Messing around where it shouldn't be."

Elena laughed. Sam was still sitting on the toilet lid, looking up at her sister. The length of Elena's neck and the point of her chin. "He isn't a raccoon, though, is he?" Elena said. "He's something we've never seen before."

As Elena walked to work, she said, she found herself hoping she would see it again. She no longer listened to music on the trail. She spent that time watching. The half hour she had to travel was private, shadowed. The only noises were the occasional car whizzing down the road and the creaking of tree branches overhead. For years, her way down that path had been a lonely routine, but now the walks were a joy because she knew something was out there with her. Something to look forward to. Something spectacular, a thing she might see that no one else who was speeding by would. A wild animal, yes. Like Sam had said. Wild and shocking and free.

"So you haven't been getting rides," Sam said.

"When I can," Elena said, "I do." But rides weren't always available. Kristine didn't have her identical schedule. Sometimes she had to go on foot.

Sam said, "I would drive you."

Elena said that wasn't her point. She asked if Sam understood what she was saying. Sam was trying her best.

Elena kept going. It was a gift, she said, to see it. She said she'd been thinking all week of what it had been like to come across it that way in the woods. Its bulk between trees. Its gaze. When it looked at her, she said, she could feel every drop of blood in her body. She felt her muscles twitching and the shape of the breath in her lungs. She felt alive—more alive than she knew was possible—like she and the bear were the only living creatures that had ever been.

Sam twisted up her mouth. "Even though it could've killed you any second."

Elena shook her head at that. "That wasn't how it was at all."

"It's a bear."

Not simply a bear, Elena said. This one was different.

Sam nodded, trying to follow. Elena went on: "He chose us." It approached them, observed them, showed with its behavior that it wished to stand alongside them. It wasn't here to hurt them.

"You're talking like you want to kiss it," Sam said. Joking. She wanted Elena to laugh at that.

"I'm not crazy."

"Oh, good," Sam said. "You could've fooled me."

Elena did laugh, then. "Am I saying anything that isn't real?" she asked. "That isn't happening?" This bear was here. It sat on their front step, practically knocking on their door. It walked to and from work beside them. It was theirs.

"It's ours," Sam repeated.

Elena exhaled. "I'm trying to be as clear as possible but I know I'm not saying this right. Sammy, when was the last time you felt really alive?"

"I'm alive right now," Sam said.

"Not like that. I'm serious. When?"

"Right now," Sam said. "With you."

Elena wasn't satisfied. Her lips thinned. She probably thought that Sam was being flippant, but Sam wasn't, Sam meant it—she did. She was aware of the flat cold under her legs and the dulled voices of the television through the wall and every odd word uttered by her sister in this room.

"Well," Elena said. "For me—it's been—it's been a hard time."

"With the bear?"

No, Elena said. Before that. For a long time before.

Sam kept listening. Elena said she wasn't complaining. It wasn't worth complaining. It was a fact, she said, things had been difficult. The regulars, her manager, the tiny tips, the occasionally docked wages. The accounts. The bills. She didn't need to get into it—it wasn't worth getting into— but obviously it had been hard, these years, Sam out of work, the pandemic, and Elena supporting them all, and Sam shouldn't try to say anything, there was nothing to say, it was just the way it was, but it had been hard, going to work every day with the weight of the household on her shoulders, fearing bringing the virus home to their mother's lungs, feeling sometimes like she couldn't keep going but knowing she had to, they needed her to, there was no way around it. The money owed on the credit cards. The question of how long they would be able to continue this way.

"I didn't know it got to you like that," Sam said.

Elena lifted her hands from the edge of the sink. "How could it not? It's exhausting. I'm exhausted. I want things to be better than this."

"I do, too," Sam said. "They will be."

"No, I know you're thinking . . . I want it now. I want to hire someone to take care of Mom during the day. But we can't afford it. Or I want it to be easier for one of us to stay home. I want her in a clinical trial where she gets better meds. I want her not to be in pain." She wasn't looking at Sam but at the floor. "I want us to feel good. I don't want to wait anymore."

"It's coming."

Elena raised her face then. Her cheeks were still damp. "No," she said. "That's what I've been telling you. It's here."

The bear, she said. The bear. It lit her days. Just hoping—knowing that she might see it—knowing it was there to be seen.

The bear had come and brought delight. The bear was deep-furred majesty. Without it, Elena didn't know what they'd do. The bear was their one good thing: a specter, a spirit, an extraordinary beast. A visitor from someplace enchanted. A vision of the mysterious world.

What had the bear done to harm them? Nothing. What threat did it pose? None at all. So why bring in someone to chase it away? There was no reason. The bear was here, briefly and beautifully, teaching them what it was to love living, helping them to make it through.

"Do you understand?" Elena asked. And Sam, sitting down, looking up, had to agree.

WHEN, TWO DAYS LATER, SAM PARKED AT HOME AFTER an early shift, she found Danny Larsen working on the front of the house. Pieces of damaged siding lay on the dirt behind him. She got out of the car and slammed the door. He turned around with a grin.

"Heard you could use some repairs," he called. At her expression, he sobered, clarified: "Elena asked me to come by."

"No, she didn't," Sam said. "She would've told me." His tools were scattered at his feet. She couldn't believe the liberties he took.

"Ah, well. Sometimes people forget to tell people stuff."

He turned to the wall before Sam could judge what he meant by that. A jab about her contacting Madeline? If Elena really had asked him to come here, did she tell him to say that? No, Sam was being paranoid, imagining this man as a messenger.

She came up the walkway and stood over his shoulder. The urine smell was faint at this point. How long had he been out here, peeling and nailing? She said, "Did you check with my mom before you started?"

"I rang the doorbell but she didn't answer. I didn't want to disturb her."

First a bear, then the sheriff, then the scientist, then this. Sam said, "I'll go find out."

Inside, her mother was resting. Sam went into her own bedroom and texted Elena, who was working and didn't answer, obviously, so Sam just messed around on her phone. She completed two more surveys before she got back up. It was uncomfortable to sit listening to someone scrape against the front of the house. It was eerily like what Elena must've heard the day she saw the bear from the living room.

Danny looked up from his work when Sam came out. "Everything okay with your mom?"

"She's fine. Also, I texted Elena," she said.

"Cool."

She sat on the front step and crossed her arms over her knees. The afternoon was breezy. The channel that morning had been thick white with fog; the railings on the deck had hardly been visible from the cabin, and when Sam went out to take her breaks, the air sat wet on her skin. Seagulls called nearby but she couldn't see them. The ferry blew its horn. When they approached a harbor, there came the sound of chains moving, the announcements to prepare to disembark, but no sign of land. Then the thump, thump of docking. The boat rocked underfoot. Tourists came on board wearing fancy rain jackets and craving cocoa. Californians, loads of them, with their weighty metal credit cards and uniform tans. She spotted Ben, once, on the car deck, laughing with the other deckhands. She hadn't tried to wave at him, and he didn't look up to see her.

Her shift had ended at eleven-thirty. The fog burned off by noon. Now there was nothing to do for the rest of the day but watch Danny push strips of vinyl under each other and nail them into place.

"It's not the right color," she said.

He studied the wall. "It was as close as I could get."

She checked her phone. Only Ben had texted: *just had lunch, galley food no good without you, missing that spice.* She texted back—*nice try, wrong though, that food's never good no matter how spicy*—and put the phone down. It buzzed again but she didn't bother looking. "When did Elena ask you to do this?"

The hammer tapped another nail in. "Yesterday."

"I didn't know you two talked." He shrugged. Sam said, "That's weird."

Danny lowered his hammer and glanced at her. "Why?"

"I don't know. It just is."

The hammer lay on his thigh. His jeans were tight on his legs. This was probably the closest she'd ever been to Danny Larsen. From this distance, she could see each twisting hair in his beard, the fine lines that years of reflexive smiles had made around his eyes. He smelled like soap. A drugstore smell. Scrubbed. He said, "These are the sorts of things neighbors do for each other."

Yeah, right. She'd never seen him making repairs at their place before. Frowning, she stared out at the road. He picked up another piece of new siding. Then he said, "I hear you all have become the place for bears to be."

Jesus Christ—so that was what was going on. He was trying to squeeze them for gossip. He must've pushed Elena into this exact conversation when she bumped into him while he was walking the dog. Smart of her, then, to put his nosiness to good use. He slotted the siding in. Sam said, "Where'd you hear that?"

Jolly, Danny said, "I have my sources." Sam rolled her eyes. He pinched a nail out of the box at his feet and added, "Steve Packenham told me. Did you know him in school?"

Sam vaguely remembered: a skinny kid, tall, with a poking-out Adam's apple. "He was your year?"

"The year above."

"What does he know about it?"

"He works for the town now." Tap, tap, tap. "Same building as the sheriff's office. They talk. He said there were markings on your house. It's been at South Beach, too. They found two dead deer down there."

Sam's heart thudded. Now she was the one who wanted to know more. "No way."

Danny sat back. "Yeah, a doe and a fawn, half-buried by the parking lot. I guess that's what a bear does, kill a thing and cache it for later."

She grimaced. "Terrible."

He picked up another strip. His hands were big, fingers

long with trimmed nails and neat cuticles. He moved like he
knew what he was doing. The siding he'd brought was cool
white, where the old strips were creamier. Maybe dirt
would make them blend together after a while.

She had to ask. "Have you seen it? The bear?"

"Me? No. You have?"

"Yeah," she said. She couldn't help it—she wanted to
tell him. "It's really scary. It's huge."

This was how these men got you. They seemed like
comfort at first. He played his part well, she had to give him
that. "You girls are brave. I would've freaked out if it
showed up at our place. Run for my gun."

"We don't have a gun."

"Even freakier."

The breeze lifted the edges of the pieces he'd discarded.
Tops of trees rustled. A bird called over them, innocent of
any predator walking the island. Sam said, "It scared me so
much."

He put his tools down again. She looked at him, then
looked away, toward the woods—she couldn't hold his eyes.
It was strange, no matter what he said, that he was here in
their yard. Looking at him was seeing double; there was his
high school self, that jock, laughing too loud and shoving
his friends, and then overlaid there was this creased-skin
man who knelt next to a box cutter and a speed square. The
younger version, she believed, wasn't to be trusted. But this
one? She couldn't reconcile the two.

"You know what else Steve told me?" Danny said. He

was speaking quietly. This was the grown-up talking, not the teen. "That we don't have anything to worry about. Bears are more scared of us than we are of them. This guy's trying to make his way over to Vancouver with as little fuss as possible."

"Right," Sam said. "That's what Elena says, too."

She glanced at him, then. His hands rested on his legs and his mouth was serious. Had she ever seen him with this face before? He looked like a different man—subdued. "Your sister is the most levelheaded person I've ever met," he said. "Listen to her. If Elena says it, then it's true."

WAS THIS WHAT ELENA MEANT, BEING ALIVE? FEELing her blood and her breath and her body? Sam and Ben fucked in the single-person bathroom on the car deck. He gripped her legs while she rode him. They were sweaty, gasping. His ID badge on its lanyard fell between them, and she pushed it over his shoulder, where his picture and his last name could thump against his back. GARCÍA, announcing itself in capital letters to nothing but the fiberglass wall. She made him take his vest off because otherwise her skin slipped against it. The reflective stripes. He left it in a ball on the floor, where his boots stuck, where thousands of other people had stepped before.

The next morning, he climbed to the top deck at fivethirty, before the galley opened to passengers, and made her come in the supply closet. She held on to the shelves of packaged pastries. She held on to his head. After her shift ended, on the ride from Anacortes back to Friday Harbor, they clawed half their clothes off together in the crew quarters. They had to be hasty there; they only had fifteen minutes between when his duties ended departing one island

and started with preparation for the next. He pressed his face into her neck, slick, warm, and pumped against her. She was alive. Wasn't she? She could feel her organs. The spot where he hit her inside. He talked to her, low and constant, saying wild things that went too far about how much he wanted her, things he would never say when they were dressed and standing a cash register's width apart, and she let the words wash over, she gripped him tighter until he collapsed. After he came, he was sweet. He nuzzled. She had to peel him off. She didn't like fucking down in quarters because his co-workers knew too much about what they were doing. When they came out, the other crew members would wink, or laugh, and Ben, still flushed, would make a joke, and she would think how dumb they all were. She'd have to go out on the deck upstairs to cool off.

Ben was cute, for a deckhand. He was fun. If this wasn't living, Sam didn't know what was. It had certainly been her whole existence so far. She'd lost her virginity to a boy in her merchant mariner course and hooked up with a couple of the caddies at the golf club. None of them stuck around; they weren't supposed to.

Elena had her own ways of getting through these years, Sam figured. Texting with Kristine. Going for walks. Organizing care for their mother. She didn't date, but she liked to hear Sam's occasional stories—the waiter from Alaska, the man who loved snorkeling, the one who kept insisting on chivalry—and so Sam liked to bring the stories (never the people) home.

For the last two months, the stories featured Ben. His parents were still in the house where he grew up, in Medford, Oregon, but he'd moved to Anacortes during lockdown. He had an associate's degree and was considering whether to go for his bachelor's. He'd asked for Sam's number the first time they met. On his days off, he fished. He could be sharp, clever, and he didn't try to trick her with kindness, and after this tourist season ended he would probably disappear, which made him exactly what Sam was looking for.

Ben gave her pleasure. He came up to the galley and sat with her at a plastic table during the late hours when few customers stopped by. She took her mask off and relaxed a little. Sometimes he pretended to read her fortune in her palm. "I see a tall, dark man in your future," he said. "About . . . ten minutes from now. In a storage closet." She pulled her hand away and rolled her eyes. Once, he brought her a jar of raspberry jam. She and Elena ate it, sweet and seedy, on their toast for days. Elena told Sam to pass on her thanks to him, but Sam didn't, and Ben didn't ask, and there were no more gifts to complicate matters after that. Instead he told her stories about his friends from home: the pranks they'd pulled, late nights with beers and drugs and firecrackers. He prompted her for her own school-days tales but she said she didn't have any.

"No stories?" he asked.

"No friends," she said.

He shook his head and called her his hermit. Asked if

everyone on her island lived alone in a cave. She said, no, just ugly little houses, and he said he'd believe that when he saw it but she'd never let him see it, and in that case he was going to picture her bearded and solitary, meditating cross-legged on the bare San Juan ground. All gaunt, he said. In a loincloth. Oh, he liked that, the loincloth— "You freak," she said then, but he said, "Who are you calling a freak, you friendless wonder?" She kicked him under the table until he grabbed her leg, gripped her ankle, ran his fingers beneath the hem of her pants.

In that way, he got her to talk about Elena. Their child-hood. On his every visit, he heard more from Sam than she intended to tell. She described their earliest walks in the woods, the clear night skies, the summer salmonberries, and he teased her through it but he also listened, he kept listening, which was in itself a satisfaction. Sam couldn't go on about her memories to anyone else; Elena already knew all these things.

They didn't only discuss the past. Ben knew her mother was sick at home, though Sam didn't get into the exact di-agnosis. And he knew Sam and Elena would be moving soon.

On the rare occasions his shift's end aligned with hers, he asked her to lunch or dinner. In Friday Harbor, in Ana-cortes. Sam always declined. The meals they did share were foods pulled from the galley: prewrapped sandwiches, na-chos topped with plasticky cheese. Later those foods would sit heavy in her stomach while he rocked into her. This was what they had together. From him, she didn't want any more.

The ferry hummed forward. The clouds gathered and parted and came together again. Ben went down to the car deck, and Sam, at her counter, organized the sweetener packets by color, pale yellow, pale pink, pale blue. Tourists complained about seasickness. Waves sloshed against the boat's sides. Toddlers ran across the cabin without supervision, until, behind Sam's back, there came the sudden noise of a slap and a shout. People bought coffee, tea, soda, kombucha. People bought cookies, chowder, soft pretzels, red apples, bananas bruised in their peels. People took sweetener by the handful. Sam organized the packets again. She had to take her enjoyment where she could find it. This period would be over soon.

Sam traveled in loops day after day—Anacortes, Orcas, Lopez, Shaw—and pictured Elena walking on the trail through the trees. She didn't picture the bear. Imagining it was too frightening—its paws crushing twigs, its breath curling from wet nostrils, its mouth open to expose yellow fangs—but imagining her sister was a balm. Elena out there, happy. Unencumbered, however briefly, by the demands of the old ladies who lunched at the club. Walking in hope of seeing something that would delight. Sam worked on accepting that image, and really, when she put her mind to it, it wasn't hard.

It shocked her, then, when Ben, loitering on her deck at quarter to nine at night, said, "Your bear is back in the news."

She'd been closing out the register. She gripped the stack of ten-dollar bills in two cold hands. "What happened?"

"Killed some lambs or something."

"Oh, God," she said. "That's terrible." Picturing the tottering black-faced things that she and Elena used to feed grass to over the fence at Hearthside Farm, while the grown sheep watched from a cautious distance. Those darlings, cached now in the clawed-open ground.

Ben didn't seem disturbed. He was sitting in one of the blue molded chairs bolted to the floor. His hair was getting long, beginning to flip over his ears, and his cheeks and neck showed stubble. He'd worked a double the day before—he looked too tired to get fussed about anything. "Everything's got to eat."

Sam put the tens down and started on the stack of fives. She didn't have to pay attention to the counting anymore. Her fingers tallied for her. "I can't believe it's still on the island. That woman said it would leave." She'd told him about Madeline.

"How long has it been?"

"Three weeks already."

"Not that long," Ben said. He stretched out his legs, pointed the toes of his boots. Sam put down the fives. "It'll go soon. You and your sister were lucky, though, weren't you?"

Once she finished the ones, she wrote the final count on a sheet and tucked it, along with the bills, into the deposit bag, then put that in the safe under the counter. All that cash, locked away, looping uselessly around the channel. "Lucky how?"

"That it didn't see you when you saw it." He pushed himself up off the chair. "It's dangerous, isn't it? Tearing into little animals." He came up behind her. Lifted his hands to her shoulders, made claws of his fingers, and pressed them there. Put his mouth against her ear. "It could've ripped you apart." Cold washed down Sam's spine. And she could feel, like Elena had described, her muscles clenching, her quick breath. She felt the whole shape of it under his fingers—this precarious life.

THE FARM WHERE THE LAMBS HAD BEEN KILLED WAS ON the north end of the island, out by Roche Harbor, but Sam's internet searches told her that bears could cover huge distances in a day, and at the grocery store she overheard a conversation about a beehive destroyed only a few miles from her family's home. The bear was a topic of interest now, as sure as news of some upstanding couple's divorce or a scandal at the annual Knowledge Bowl. It was something the good citizens of Friday Harbor came together over. A communal conversation.

As far as Sam could hear, no one had anything of real value to say. There'd been no sightings half as substantial as hers and Elena's. Nobody had yet gotten a good picture of the thing. People were gossiping over a paw print here, a pile of scat there. They talked about the bear like it was the island's exotic pet. A new mascot, to replace the image of the snarling wolverine stuck to the side of the high school. It scared them, but more than that it excited them, the way riding a red coupe over San Juan's hills might—it gave them a story of adventure to tell each other tire-lessly.

Sam heard them in the clinic, the pharmacy, the general store. On the ferry, even, a tourist family approached her to ask if she knew where on the island they might spot bears. To tell the truth, she'd heard that before—tourists asked the stupidest things—but this time the question didn't seem like simple geographic misunderstanding. Everyone wanted to see it. The magic Elena had talked about, they wanted to be part of that.

Sam just went to work and waited for the animal to van-ish. She and Elena had gotten through their encounters with it more or less untouched; a little fear, a little humilia-tion, a quick and bewildering disagreement, but now they were fine. The house was damaged but Elena had arranged for that to be taken care of. Their family made it through with minimal loss of money or time. Sam didn't want to risk either any further. Let the bear be everyone else's dis-traction now. Sam was only thinking of what would have to happen beyond it: the day a buyer came to the property without any worry of smelling musk.

The whole situation had gone to show how much she and Elena needed to get off this island. Sam wanted to be somewhere big enough to have more than one subject dis-cussed at the drugstore. She wanted more than one drug-store. She wanted more. So when, toward the end of her morning shift, she learned the afternoon galley worker had called out, she told her manager without hesitation that she could cover. Getting paid time and a half for boiling water: yes, she could do that. No problem. She texted Elena to let her know.

Overtime was an opportunity but also a sacrifice. By her twelfth hour on the clock, the minutes crawled. It was late afternoon before a crew member came up to say they'd found someone else to take the rest of the shift. Sam offered to stay later—she was already halfway through eternity— but the crew member waved his hands to dismiss her. Centerplate didn't feel like paying her rate after all, Sam supposed. The new girl boarded at Lopez and stepped into Sam's station. For her last twenty minutes on the boat that day, Sam rode out in the open air, letting fine mist wash across her face. Seaplanes hummed overhead.

She drove home from the harbor with the windows down. The breeze was warm, powdery with pollen, soft with the promise of early summer. Here was another day she'd almost entirely missed, penned through the daylight hours in the fluorescent-lined box on the ferry's top deck, but she'd made it at last into this sunshine. Driving lazily, playing pop on the radio. Trees brushed by on either side. Farm animals watched her pass. When she and Elena moved off-island, they would enjoy, she imagined, mentioning to people the beautiful place in which they'd grown up. The air smelled like cedar and sugar. It was lovely. With every curve in the road, her body relaxed deeper into the driver's seat. She'd gotten the final piece of the day, the sliver of goodness left.

At the side of the road, the edge of the shoulder: Elena. Sam spotted her as she passed. Elena's back to the cars, her hair up, her telltale black polo from the club. Sam checked the time and the rearview mirror and then pulled off, a quick right onto gravel, and turned in her seat to see. Yes, definitely. She stuck her head out the window to call— "Elena!"—but she was just a fraction too far away for her sister to hear. Sam spun the wheel, swung across the road, and drove back to pull over by where her sister stood.

They were less than twenty feet from each other now. Sam leaned across the passenger seat. "El," she shouted, but her sister didn't turn around. Sam tapped the horn, one polite beep, and Elena startled, and something beyond her, some enormous low shadow, moved.

Sam knew what it was. She knew. Was this how their mother felt? In her chest, all the time? Their mother, whose lungs were failing, whose arteries strained and would soon collapse—was this how their mother sat with the knowledge of death? How sure it was. Sam's own certainty took her breath away, too.

Elena shaded her eyes with her hand and grinned. She shone in the sunlight. There had been a bear behind her. Sam had seen it. A bear beside her sister, close enough to walk over to and touch.

AS SOON AS ELENA WAS SAFELY IN THE CAR, SAM SAID, "What the fuck was that." Quick as she could, she locked the doors. Elena was pulling down her seatbelt to buckle. Through the glass rising in the window frame, the trees stood motionless.

"You're off late," Elena said. "What was what?"

"Was that what I thought it was?" It was, it was.

"Was what?" Elena was playing games with her. She was smiling, bantering. She smelled like the grill and like something else. Dirt. The woods. Oh, God, Sam's heart. "What did you think it was?"

"Elena," Sam said. "Stop. A fucking bear. That's what. I just saw you with it right there."

Elena kept smiling. That beloved canine, her teeth precise and sweet. The bags under her eyes were dark, thin-skinned, but creased up and almost hidden by her happiness. "Okay. So?"

Inside Sam, a violence rose. She flung her hand off the steering wheel and grabbed her sister's shoulder. Dug into it with five fingers. All her might. Elena twisted under her grip and said, "Stop it," but Sam wasn't letting go, and Elena said, *"SAM,"* and took her own hands and pried at Sam's, ripped her away. Her fingernails into Sam's wrist, puncturing the back of Sam's hand, leaving crescent-moon marks red and purple in Sam's skin. That bite, that shock. Sam hit at her, tried to get her, and Elena swatted her away. Elena's body thumped against the passenger-side door. Sam's seatbelt caught and tugged her backwards. Sam hit again at air.

Elena was shouting. Desperate. "What are you doing?"

"What am *I* doing?" Sam shouted back. "What—" The seatbelt had locked in place, restraining her. She hit against the wheel and the horn blasted. She pounded on it. There was some satisfaction in the noise: the scream louder than she could scream, the greatest possible disruption. It would keep the animals away. She kept going.

Their car was filled with noise. Her mind was obliterated by it. Her fingers hurt, her jaw ached, two of the moon marks on the back of her right hand were filled bloody. Her sister. What was she thinking. Right there.

Elena reached out, cupped a hand over Sam's, and pulled it off the wheel. Moving slowly. "Sammy."

So gentle, Sam thought. Like taming a beast.

"Shh," Elena said. "Take a breath."

Sam let her head drop against the headrest. Her ears were ringing. The violence had receded as suddenly as it'd come, leaving emptiness in its wake. Worn out by what had flooded over, Sam shut her eyes. She pulled air in through her nose.

"You hit me," Elena said. "You can't do that. It's not acceptable."

Sam lifted her head again. "I'm sorry," she said, automatically, truthfully—who was she, their mother's ex? She wasn't that kind of person, able to hurt someone. The impulse had simply come over her.

Elena squeezed her hand, then reached over to shut off the engine. "If you want to talk about it, let's talk about it," she said. "But you and I don't act that way."

"I just—" Sam didn't know where to start. "What were you doing?"

"Nothing."

"No, not nothing—"

Elena said, "I was saying hello."

The body that had withdrawn back into the tree line. Its shocking size. "You were . . . what?"

"Sometimes, not always, but sometimes, on my way to and from work, he's there. And if he is, he comes over. I say hi. I talk to him."

"You talk to him."

"He listens. If I have a snack with me, he'll want it."

Sam could not believe what she was hearing. "That's literally exactly what we're not supposed to do."

"It doesn't happen that often."

"This is insane," Sam said. "Can you hear yourself? You're being insane."

Elena sighed. She was making expressions like she was exasperated with Sam—as if Sam hadn't potentially saved her life by pulling the car over—as if Sam somehow wasn't seeing the situation clearly. "Okay, you don't understand," she said, and that in itself was a blow. Sam wanted to understand. She had been trying to understand. If there was some aspect of this she didn't, at this point, grasp, it was because Elena had kept its details from her. "Do you really think I would do anything crazy? I'm only standing there. And he's learning me, getting to know how I behave. It's like— you know how a dog sniffs your hand before it lets you pet it?"

"Are you *petting* it?"

Elena took another breath. "I need you to listen to me. Right now you aren't listening at all."

Sam couldn't stand the sound of her sister's measured inhalations and exhalations. The place in her where fury had risen before felt empty and enormous. It was the distance between her and Elena. It shouldn't exist. She didn't want to be strapped here, misunderstanding, a center console's width from Elena and on opposite sides of an abyss. She wanted to be together with her sister as they ought to be.

Sam needed to close this gap between them. She said to Elena, "Tell me again."

"I walk to work and back, like always. I look for him. Sometimes he's there. If he does approach, I stand, arms by my sides, and let him however near he wants to come. I'm not doing anything to provoke him." Elena was being patient. She was making her words as precise and soothing as possible, because she wanted to be united, too. "I know," she said, "that they told us not to give food. They tell us those warnings so we stay away from animals that are aggressive or unpredictable, except he's not either. He's different. They talk about bears in general—they say they act this way and do these things. But they don't know this one. He has his own personality, like you or I do. He's not like what they say."

Sam was trying her best to absorb this. "What's his . . . personality?"

Elena thought. "He's very gentle. He doesn't rush. He's curious."

Sam sat. She had to think, too. It was true that no one so far, not the sheriff's deputies or the *Journal* reporters, the state scientist or the people whispering at the grocery store, had told the sisters anything that matched their actual experience. They said the bear was small, but it was huge; they called it black, but it was vivid brown; they said it would leave the island, and it had not. What everyone else described was not the thing Sam and Elena had seen sitting at their door.

Elena was right: what was going on here was exceptional. A fairy-tale creature stepping out of the trees. Madeline Pettit had warned against approaching the animal, but she hadn't said what to do if the animal came to them, held itself like a tame thing, snuffled and sniffed. She hadn't even considered the possibility. So Elena was right: something outside those authorities' knowledge was happening. Something one of a kind.

The child in Sam, the little-sister part that would always, no matter how old they were or where they lived, be there, absorbed this. Elena, herself, was special. Their whole family was not like the neighbors they'd known. It made a certain fundamental sense that different things, things that could not be related to by others, would happen to them.

Sam's attention was entirely on Elena. The tiny muscles in Elena's cheeks and her dry quiet lips. The untweezed hairs under her brows. Her eyes, her neck, her jawline. The insulated air between them—the warmth the car trapped. Their mingled smells. Soil, salt water, hamburger grease, and creased dollar bills. All Sam's thoughts, every sense at her command, were taking in Elena. Giving over to Elena. Her sister was asking her to accept the impossible, but it was only the impossible reality in which they already lived.

"Okay," Sam said.

"Okay?"

"Okay." Sam turned the key in the ignition. The car chimed. She touched her sister's shoulder, the one she'd seized before. "Sorry."

"It's all right," Elena said. "The whole thing is . . . intense."

Sam held the steering wheel. She had to laugh. "It is." Looking over her shoulder, she made another U-turn and started driving home.

Elena put her window down and Sam did the same. Wind flowed across them, tousling their hair, filling their ears. The road was mostly empty of other cars. The farther Sam and Elena got from the center of Friday Harbor, the more peaceful things became. Their house was only a few miles from town but felt like another universe. It was a place without tourists or ferries or galleries or boutiques or oat-milk lattes or stuffed souvenir octopuses. A place that was quiet, lush with new summer growth, entirely theirs.

"I know you think I don't understand," Sam said, "but I do." She turned right off Cattle Point.

Elena was chastened by that. Sam, watching the road, could hear it in her sister's voice. "No, I know you do."

"And I'm trying to be helpful to you."

"I know you are."

"It's just hard to sort out," Sam said. "Obviously. It's this totally unprecedented situation." They were already pulling up in front of the house. The thick green of the trees in the yard, the scattered dirt, the shabby siding. Their mother in there, waiting. Sam put the car in park, touched the dangling keys, and gathered herself. She turned to her sister once more. Elena: whom she'd hit, whom she loved. "All I want is for you to be happy."

In the passenger seat, Elena, still seatbelted, sank with relief. It was startling for Sam to see, how marked the effect was. Her shoulders dropped and her eyelids lowered.

"Thank you," she said. "I really needed to hear that from you."

"It's true," Sam said. "I'll tell you anytime. You know what I was thinking about? Remember that video of the guys hugging a lion?" Elena shook her head. "Oh," Sam said. "Well, it was cool." A classmate had shown it to Sam in the elementary school library. She remembered, precisely, the fuzzy yellow quality of the images, the swelling music as the lion ran full speed across African savanna and leapt into a thin man's arms. It had brought tears to Sam's eyes. Bizarre as they were, these situations weren't unknown: Sam had seen television shows where characters befriended elephants, movie trailers about men in Canada who lived with grizzlies, and pictures in books of people cuddling gorillas. She'd been told myths of orphans and wolf packs and beauties and beasts. Thousands of years before, people living in caves had drawn these creatures on their walls to dance in the fire around them while they slept. Somewhere, somehow, in the space left unexplored by bureaucrats and biologists, there existed possibilities. There might be magic to be found.

Home was waiting. They would have chicken thighs for dinner. Elena reached for her door handle but didn't pull it yet. "I love you," she said.

"I love you."

"You trust me?"

"Always," Sam said. "Yes. You know I do."

Elena's smile returned. She used to look like this when they were girls adventuring. Unencumbered. She would lead them deep into the woods. Sam smiled back. It was irresistible. Elena said, "Listen, Sammy, do you want to meet him, too?"

A ND SO SAM FOUND HERSELF, ON HER NEXT DAY OFF, after an afternoon of tidying the house and buying eggs and refilling their mother's prescriptions and pulling a hair clog from the slow-draining shower, parked in the golf club's lot. Electric vehicles glided into the spaces around her. Sam couldn't think about what she and Elena were about to do; she couldn't help thinking about it; she stared up, out the windshield, over the rolling hills of the green and the white boxes of golf carts, to the clouds turning slowly across pure blue.

Elena flung open the passenger-side door and Sam jumped. Climbing in, Elena laughed, and Sam laughed, too, shaky, starting the car. "How was work?"

"Shitty," Elena said. "It doesn't matter. Ready?"

As ready as she could be. They drove together around the manicured perimeter of the club, covering in minutes the distance that took an hour of Elena's day to walk. Golfers raised clubs against the sky. The car had filled with the smell of the grill. Did the bear follow Elena because of that smell? Seasoned meat.

"Pull over," Elena said.

Sam guided their car off the road. Its weight rolled across gravel, soil, and matted grass before coming to a stop. They were a ten-minute walk from the spot on the trail where the bear had first approached Elena, two weeks earlier. Surrounding them were trees shot through with sunlight. Brown rippled trunks and the thin glistening lines of spiderwebs. Leaves swaying. Sam turned off the engine.

She dreaded this. No, she craved it. Both. She was terrified and fascinated and daunted by what was to come. She wanted to talk to her sister but she didn't know what to say. Elena was climbing out of her seat. Sam followed.

Elena was already beyond the slope of the road's shoulder, but Sam, coming around from the driver's side, had to slide a few feet down. The ground was soft and uneven under her shoes. Elena was at the trees; immediately, she was striped with shadow, turned brown and blue as a bruise. Sam, crossing the tree line, felt the temperature shift of shadow on her own skin. She hurried after.

Across the road from where they'd pulled over, an unpaved driveway broke the line of the forest, but it wasn't visible now. The slope up to the road and the branches above blocked it. They were heading away from human habitation, toward whatever else waited. And Elena had started calling. Calm, clear, her voice rose into the air: "Are you there? Hello? I'm here. Can you hear me?"

The confidence of Elena's words. The way they shivered, precise as a ringing bell, into the woods. The sound

made Sam tremble. One day, in their future lives, this would
be a crazy story they told each other; one day, Sam would
repeat these words to Elena to jog her memory and to amuse.

Hello? Are you there?
I'm here. Can you hear me?
Hello? Are you there? I'm here.
Can you hear me? Hello? I'm here. Are you there?
I'm here. Hello? Are you there?

They were far enough in now that the road, their car,
and any help were out of sight. The ground was thick with
moss. Elena stepped over fallen logs. The bear, if it was listening, could approach from any direction. Sam slipped on
a slick patch of mud and caught herself. She took an extra
step to catch up with her sister. Prayed nothing was on its
way.

I'm here. Hello? Can you hear me? Are you there?
Hello? Are you there?
I'm here.

Elena said she used to have dreams about animals attacking them. Sam couldn't remember any of her own, but she
felt their residue, the terror of childhood nightmares. Shark
attacks and serial killers. Chases into a witch's lair. These
were the woods she knew, the same ones she'd walked all
her life, but they were changed by the creature that had

come into them. They frightened her. Her breath was short, her pulse throbbing in her neck, and she couldn't tell if that was caused by her stumbling over caked leaves or by what she imagined. She was almost made faint by the pictures Elena's words put in her head. She did not want to be here.

An arm's length ahead, Elena stopped walking. She lifted her chin. Sam reached her side, and Elena glanced over at her. Winked.

Wasn't this like a dream, too: Elena's familiarity, her foreignness. Her sister and yet not her sister. An altered girl. Sam could smell the earth, the sap, the sharp crushed flakes of bark underfoot. The saliva-thickening weight of mud, the floury dust of pollen. Birds chirped. The breeze blew. She could smell something rotten.

The bear had arrived.

Elena looked out to their right and Sam looked after. There. Moving, an enormous animal, coming toward them. Its head was huge. Its arms were broad and its shoulders were high, an alternating rise with every step, one blade lifted then the other. Its back dipped then rose again into a wide rump. The bear moved in a slow arc around them. It watched.

Sam didn't exhale. Elena said, "Oh, hello, there."

The bear was less than fifty feet away now. Almost directly in front of them. Furred and muscle-bound.

"This is my sister," Elena said. "I wanted you to meet each other."

The bear slowed to a stop. It waited. Deliberate, Sam thought, it was being deliberate, it was deliberating.

Elena laughed, then, a sound that could not have surprised Sam more. Elena was totally relaxed. Her voice, the easy swing of it, was intimate—it suggested friendship. How many times had she seen this thing? Did she find it here every day? "Hungry, hungry," she said. "I don't have anything for you this time."

Sam could hear the air exiting its monstrous lungs. It raised its head. Then, in one fluid motion, it stood, lifting its great weight off its arms and straightening its spine.

Sam thought: *now*. Now it would lunge forward. Now was when they would die.

The bear stood there on its short hind legs. Its belly was thick with pale yellow fur. It looked at them, appraising. Its arms hung at its sides. Its neck was massive.

Elena had told Sam that the bear was something extraordinary. She said it was magic—enchanted—a gift from the animal gods— She'd told Sam, leading up to this afternoon, that when she was with it she felt strong and brave and also tiny and insignificant and utterly aware of her own body and dissolved into everything else in the universe. She felt glowing and connected and magnificent. She told Sam that this was the best thing that had ever happened—she said that. Elena. That the bear was what she looked forward to each day. And Sam, even in her fear, crossing into this forest, had come because she believed she might feel that too.

She didn't. She was horrified.

Different, yes; Elena had been right about that; Sam was hit with a feeling she did not have any other moment of her day. This was different from sex, from dreaming, from counting out tips, from the routine devastation of doctors' visits. It was not like driving winding roads or listening to loud music. It was not sleeping late or riding the ferry through the fog. It was something else entirely. It was standing before a bear. The only other feeling that had ever gotten close was when she was fourteen years old and Elena was fifteen and their mother's boyfriend lived with them, and they would hear him coming down the hall toward their bedroom and then he would open their door, and there was nothing they could do about him, his rage, there was no one to protect them. It was like that, except it was worse.

Sam was not strong or brave or tiny or aware. She didn't dissolve into an appreciation of the intricate links in the food chain. This was not wonderful. She was only herself, acutely, and certain that she did not want to die this way. She did not want to be clawed, eviscerated, decapitated. She didn't want her life to end on San Juan. This creature could not come any closer to her. She wanted it to get away.

The bear kept standing there staring. It was bigger than a refrigerator. Brown tinged with gold. Its fur was heaped shaggy around its throat, at its armpits, and over its groin. The animal's stink was overwhelming: old urine, wet dog. It was near enough for Sam to see its nostrils flare. It was huffing them in.

Elena asked, "Do you want to say hi?"

Sam was silent. Elena touched Sam's wrist. Reflexively, Sam clenched her fists, and the bear's eyes tracked Sam's movement. Two amber beads tugged on a string.

Elena said, "Well?"

Sam tried to speak without moving her lips. "Me?"

"Yes, you. Who else would I be asking, him?"

Would that be such a surprise? Elena had been talking to the animal like it was her companion this whole time. Still, Sam attempted, mere feet from destruction, to act like this was fine. "Okay," she said. She looked at the bear, and the bear looked at her, its eyes glass, its expression unreadable. It didn't have an expression. It was not human. It had no thoughts, only the instinct to devour them. With her sister waiting beside her, Sam said, "Hi."

"He's curious about you," Elena said.

Sam made a noise.

"Remember what that woman said? He stands like that when he wants to find out more."

Sam was going to go to her death like this: trying to humor her sister, making small talk with a beast. The bear was going to drop to all fours, push off the dirt toward them, and launch teeth-first into her neck. It was going to rip her apart. She was going to bleed.

To the bear, Elena said, "You didn't bother any more livestock, did you? You wild thing."

It turned its gaze toward her. Elena chuckled, pleased, clearly, to have its attention again. Sam felt cold. She was frozen and stiff and profoundly aware of how stupid they were being. Playing at friendship with something that had no capacity to care for them.

The bear fell forward. Its front paws hit the earth. Sam jolted. *Now.*

On all fours, it stretched its mouth wide open. Its lips slid over its teeth, exposing red-white gums and yellow bone. Its tongue lolled out. It shifted its weight, and then it turned from them to walk slowly away. Elena called after: "See you soon."

Then Elena turned to Sam. The bear's body was still visible, weaving through the trees. Leaving them? Or circling them? "What'd you think?" Elena said.

Sam said, "Let's get to the car."

Elena was grinning. "No, hold on," she said, "I want to hear what you think. Incredible, isn't he?"

Sam was in the dream again. The horrible realm entered in the middle of the night where her house was different and intruders were breaking in and Elena was not Elena anymore. Sam couldn't recognize this. She couldn't bear it. She had to wake up and return to her old expected life, where they were pressured and even at times desperate but they were always, at the very least, safe. She said, "Mom's waiting for us." She took Elena's warm arm in her hands. Sam was trembling. She was begging. "Let's get back to the car. Now. Please."

ELENA MADE DINNER FOR THEIR MOTHER THAT EVE-
ning but Sam had to excuse herself to lie down. She
felt ill, she told them. It was true, she did. The day had sick-
ened her. Lying in bed, she kept seeing her sister—the animal focusing on her. Those round eyes glowing. Lit yellow
from within. The thick shag of its fur, so deep you could
lose your hand in it. Elena, defenseless, in front.

Sam opened up a survey. Tapped her way through two
pages.

The questions weren't settling her. She had done varia-
tions of them a million times before—age, gender, race,
ethnicity, zip code, household income, favorite breakfast
foods—but they weren't numbing quickly enough now.
While picking her answers, she saw Elena. The bear's claws,
horrifically long, gripping the dirt, and Elena's sneakered
feet on the forest floor.

The phone buzzed with a text from Ben. Sam couldn't
take his banter in this moment. She swiped her way over to
her browser instead. Looking up humans and animals, she
found an article about a man who had kept a full-grown al-

ligator in his bathtub. He ended up in prison for reckless endangerment. One woman who tried to befriend a chimpanzee had her arms and face ripped off. Elephants trampled a woman in India, then showed up at her funeral to trample her casket again. The man from the movie trailer who'd moved north to live with grizzlies had been mauled, along with his girlfriend, to death.

Was she going to throw up? Her mouth was wet and sour. Beyond her door, she could hear her family's voices. Why, why, had Sam gone along with what Elena told her about this situation? In the kitchen, in the bathroom, in the car. Why had Sam let herself be convinced? Did she have to agree with absolutely every word Elena ever said?

Before any allegiance to her older sister could interfere, Sam thumbed over to her email and brought up the thread with Madeline. She typed fast: *Hi. What's the best way for us to make sure we're safe from the bear coming near us? Thanks.* Sent.

As soon as the email was off, the guilt flooded in. Sam pressed her phone to her chest and stared at the cracked ceiling. She'd had to do it, she told herself. This had become a matter of survival. She couldn't hesitate because she thought Elena might be mad. And besides, Elena had only made her promise not to bring Madeline to the house, which Sam wasn't, so she wasn't making more problems, she wasn't doing anything wrong. She had only asked a question, the answer to which they needed to know.

This reasoning wasn't helping. Out in the hall, a door

shut. Footsteps. Elena was humming. Sam still felt sick. She had to calm herself, so she lay there, shut her eyes, and thought her favorite thoughts: the ones of a future where there was nothing to fear.

Five hundred thousand dollars. Once they got themselves and the car off the island, they'd have all that money to do what they liked. First, from the port, they'd drive south along I-5. They would cross the Skagit River, thick with evergreens on both shores. The radio would be loud, and the smell of pine would be everywhere. They'd pass the Skagit Wildlife Area, where thousands of snow geese stood shoulder to shoulder in the winter, and Possession Sound, where gray whales fed every spring.

They'd get a hotel in Seattle and stay there for a few days, or a week, or, if they really liked it, housekeeping and continental breakfasts, forever. If not, they could rent a luxury apartment. Someplace glass-walled, with a doorman and a parking garage. Each of them would have her own bathroom, so Sam could leave her eyeliner pencils scattered on her vanity and Elena could drape a used washcloth over her sink faucet, and it wouldn't matter, there'd be no cause to bicker. In the evening, from their sofa, they'd look out onto a new horizon as a million lights flickered on.

Or if they didn't like the city, that packed urban lifestyle, they could keep driving. South to Tacoma? East to Yakima? West to the Olympic Peninsula? They would hike the Hoh Rain Forest, summit Mount Rainier, soak at the Sol Duc Hot Springs. For once, they would be the tourists, and someone else would fetch them coffee—Sam and Elena would tip a hundred percent on every check. If they got tired of Washington, they would go to Idaho. California. Up to mainland Canada, where their mother had traveled as a child, but the sisters themselves had never been. Sam and Elena would go dancing and drink cocktails and get passports. They would have no connection but each other to who they used to be.

Sam didn't have every step of the plan decided, but she was sure of one thing: how good they would feel. The bear would be nothing to Elena once they got out of here. The lines under her eyes would go away. They'd wake up late, they wouldn't work. When they were hungry, they'd eat at restaurants, order multiple courses, taste things without the obligation to clear their plates. Whenever their rooms got dirty, they'd hire a cleaner. Someone else would grocery shop on their behalf. Sam would go on dates. Elena would take up skiing. They would do whatever they wanted every second for the rest of their lives.

Sam's breathing slowed. The house was quiet. Outside her bedroom window, the sky was deep dark blue. She got up.

Their mother's door was closed. Her oxygen was on. In the velvet black of the hallway, Sam traced her fingers along the walls. The bathroom door was ajar, and light from the rising moon trickled in through the window. Sam moved in shadow toward the front of the house.

Wood eased under her feet. One step creaked. Another.

She went as quietly as she could toward the living room, which was bled through with night. The glass in the windows caught thin starlight. The curtain around where her sister slept hung motionless.

Elena had told Sam that the bear was special. But what Elena didn't seem to understand was that she, herself, was the special thing.

If Elena were awake right now, Sam would kneel next to her and plead with her to see that. She would say, Elena, we're so close to what we've waited for. I know it's been too long—years longer than we thought—and it's been hard on you, all this responsibility, it's too much. It's exhausting, you said; you're exhausted. I know that. Me too. But, Elena, we're almost there. Hold on.

We don't need this animal. It's not worth the risk. If you crave quick relief, get it elsewhere—eat candy or get drunk or drive fast. Cut your hair short, if you like; I love your hair, it's perfect, but you can change it, dye it purple, Mom would do it for you, it'd be fun. Indulge yourself. But don't go into the woods for this thing anymore.

Don't do this. That's what Sam would say. Bent in the dark, in their home, face-to-face with her sister. Cracking open with fear and with faith. Elena. Please. We have each other. We'll make it through this. Elena, can't you hold on to that, and let the bear go?

Sam woke up late the next morning. Her bedroom was flooded by sun. The walls, which were painted pale orange, sherbet color, were suffused with light. Radiant.

Elena was gone for work, but Sam's shift didn't start until noon. She went to the bathroom to drink from the tap. Her mouth was tacky, tongue dry, and throat rough. Had she been sobbing in her sleep? She felt wrung out. Eyes aching, she headed to her mother's room, where she found her mother watching some game show.

"Have you already had breakfast?" Sam asked.

Her mother shook her head. "Elena made me a bowl, but I wasn't hungry. She left it in the fridge."

The TV made Sam's head ache. People jumping up and down in front of buzzer stations. "Are you hungry now? I can bring it."

Her mother picked up the remote, turned the volume down, and pushed her blanket back. "I'll come."

They moved along the hall together. Sam walked behind her mother, keeping watch. The bones on the back of her mother's neck stood out as high ridges. Topography of a desolate land. Her ankles were swollen. Behind them, the faint sounds of the show continued: cheering and a host's happy voice.

"You okay?" Sam asked.

Her mother had one hand out for balance. "I'm good."

Once her mother took a seat in the kitchen, Sam pulled the leftover oatmeal from the refrigerator to reheat in the microwave. She mixed syrup into it as it steamed. At her mother's request, she made coffee, too—Elena wouldn't like that, was always trying to get their mother to have herbal tea. They ate together at the table while the sun poured in.

"How are you doing, baby?" her mother asked.

Sam didn't know where to start. Elena had introduced her to a bear the day before. She'd spent the last night having visions of alligators and chimpanzees. "Fine," Sam said, taking out her phone to refresh her email: nothing yet from Madeline. Quick, she tapped a text to Elena: *You get to work ok this morning?* Sending the text made her fear surface, sharp as a fang. What if the answer was no?

"How is it being back on the boat? Are there as many summer people as there used to be?"

Sam looked up. "It's okay," she said. "Not as busy as before, but the season's still early. We'll see."

"Do most of them wear masks?"

"Not really." The phone vibrated under Sam's palm and she glanced down. Elena had replied: *Yeah totally. Why?*

"You know what I'd love to do this summer?" her mother said. "Now that the world's opening back up? Take a trip to Vancouver Island. What do you think, maybe the next time you girls both have the day off, we could go over, walk around Sidney, have afternoon tea at a hotel?"

Absently, Sam said, "They stopped running the ferry there when the pandemic started." She wrote, *Thinking about you*. On the screen there was no sign of Elena's typing back. Sam wrote again: *Worrying*

Why?

Guess

Ha, Elena sent. Then: *No worries. All good*

Her mother said, "I miss having you here all day. I got used to it."

Sam looked up. Her mother's lips were blue-tinged. Her eyes were large and lovely. "Oh," Sam said. "I did, too, Mom. I miss it, too." The last two years of staying home, doing chores, and waiting for life to begin. Sam and her mother fitting their meals around Elena's work schedule because there was nothing else to look forward to. Virtual doctors' visits that missed her mother's every important symptom. The claustrophobia of it all—the closeness.

"The shows aren't the same without you watching along."

"Yeah. You've got to keep me updated on what's happening."

"Who knows. I lose track of it," her mother said. "I get so bored."

Sam laughed. "You know what? At work, me too." Her mother smiled wide. Those perfect front teeth. She was still the prettiest. She touched Sam's hand, the one holding the phone, with cold fingertips.

What was it in Elena and in their mother that drew toward danger? Looking at them, Sam could not make sense of it. They were the type of women who ought to need no one, and whom everyone wished to be around. Sam and Elena's grandmother, too, had been like that—self-assured, in their mother's stories of her. A nurse, a flirt, a tender of the vegetable garden that once grew by the side of their house, before things got too busy and the plants withered away. But their grandfather used to have rages, their mother told them. He smashed plates and punched open their walls. Their grandmother, as capable as she seemed in their mother's telling, had put up with his violences for years. She'd had three children with him. When he totaled the family car, she got a bicycle. Those were the memories their mother liked to share: how dazzling her mother had been on a bike, cruising along the island roads with her hair blowing behind.

Their grandmother hadn't gotten out from the threat of him until he died. For a brief window, she, their mother, Elena, and Sam lived together in this house, squeezed tight, their precious family, and then their grandmother passed. Eventually their mother brought destruction back in.

When their mother's boyfriend started living with them, Sam thought of him every second. In class, after school, while he worked, as she and Elena fell asleep—he constantly had to be negotiated. Was he in a good mood? If not, how could they repair things for him—or stay out of his way? What did their mother need them to do, at dinner or while he watched TV, to set things right? He had countless rules that Sam and Elena always ended up breaking. Their mother did, too. They tried so hard but he never found their efforts enough.

Their house was small and he could set the whole thing shaking. They lived like that for nearly a year before Social Services stepped in. He moved out, and these days, Sam went weeks, months, without a thought of his being there. He entered her head only randomly: if she overheard an argument between two strangers, or passed some man who used his same cologne. On those instances she happened to brush too close to someone broad-shouldered and overly friendly. When her mother brought up the past. Though they never talked about him, she occasionally mentioned the period that had overlapped with him. Its terrors.

But marks faded. Nobody flinched anymore. His only meaningful effect was that, afterward, the members of their family knew to what end each could and could not be counted on. Their mother would, if offered, eat a poisoned apple, while the sisters would not. They didn't love their mother any less for that quality—she had inherited it, a curse laid on her family line. They just put some distance between themselves and her after that. They grew up to pursue a world beyond such threats.

So Sam had thought, anyway. Until her sister started to call to the bear.

"You girls work so hard," her mother said. "Do you know how proud I am of you?"

Sam stirred her oatmeal. It was congealing on the sides of the bowl. "We learned from the best."

From the back of the house, a voice actor recited the side effects of some advertised medication. Her mother chewed. "Do you think you and Elena will raise your own kids here?"

Sam coughed against her spoon. The whole notion—no. Eight years ago, Sam had somehow gotten pregnant (which didn't make sense, she always used protection, and yet she'd ended up conceiving a year earlier than their mother did with Elena) and Elena had taken her to the health center in town. They'd sat together there, waiting for someone to come in with an abortion referral. Sam had felt queasy. That was her lasting impression of her short pregnancy: the constant feeling of car sickness. And disappointment. In the office, which was decorated with framed watercolors of the ocean to try to look serene, Elena squeezed Sam's knee and said, "We're going to get through this."

Then the nurse came in. Sam got her pills, her blood, her clean slate. She got renewed resolve to avoid the ways a place might trap its residents: teen pregnancy, marriage to a high school sweetheart, a gaggle of girlfriends who met monthly at a bar, a decision to accept the shitty hand you'd been dealt. Sam and Elena weren't going to do any of that. Not ever.

"I don't know about that," Sam said to her mother.

"It means a lot to picture babies in this house again. Your

mimi would've loved that. She was so excited when she found out Elena was on the way."

"She wasn't mad?" Sam asked.

Her mother looked at her, quick and stunned at the question. "Why would she be?"

"You were so young."

"I wasn't a child. I'd already been working for ages." The coffee mug had left a brown ring on the table. Sam fetched a dishcloth to wipe it up. Her mother went on. "You two were a gift. One right after the other. You don't argue with the timing of gifts, do you? You don't say, oh, no, not right now, I'm not ready. You open your arms and welcome them."

Sam folded the cloth and set it under the mug. She could think of an argument or two against that.

"Are you seeing anyone?" her mother asked.

"Come on," Sam said, embarrassed.

Her mother was being playful. "I'm just asking."

"No. No one."

"What about Elena?"

Oh, Elena's seeing something, Sam imagined saying. A creature that stalks her along the side of the road. A thing that comes out of the woods to sniff her. A wild animal.

"You know how Elena is," Sam said. "Nope."

Her mother passed her bowl, a layer of oatmeal thick on its bottom, to Sam, who got up to put it in the sink. Her back to the table, she checked her phone again. One new

email. A response from Madeline Pettit. Sam held her
breath.

> Hi Sam, thanks for getting in touch. Is this a hypo-
> thetical question? If so, I want to reiterate that it is
> very unlikely any bear would approach you. That
> said, if this one does, you can clap your hands and
> yell to scare him off. Carrying a safety whistle and/or
> bear deterrent spray can also help provide peace of
> mind. Best, M

Bear spray. Sam checked the time on the microwave:
there wasn't going to be time to shop for it before work.
She'd slept too late, she'd fucked up the whole thing, she'd
have to wait. Her mother, she realized, was still talking.
Sam took the coffeepot from the counter, filled both their
mugs, and sat back down.

"These days, you don't even need a man to have a baby,"
her mother said. "People can get pregnant at the doctor's
office. You pick what kind you want out of a catalog. And
once it's born, things work out."

"Mom. Oh my god."

"I'm just saying."

"Stop saying it!" Sam was trying to sound jokey in return, but under her words was shrill humiliation. Her
mother was bringing up subjects that she herself, if she were
thinking reasonably, would not want to discuss. Things

work out, she'd said. Had they for her? An orphan with two toddlers by the time she was twenty-five?

Her mother leaned forward. Her expression was sober now. Sometimes Sam thought her mother didn't know what was going on with them, but other times she found a person who listened, even to what wasn't said. In this house, there were countless secrets kept simply to protect each other; their mother, every so often, picked one up as it hummed through the air.

Her voice was soft. "Only thinking how I'd like to meet my grandchildren."

So her mother hadn't heard what was buzzing in Sam's head. The bear, the fears, the need to escape these island deaths that waited for them. Well. Why should she? What she'd said was clarifying even so: their time together was short. Even if Elena and Sam both got pregnant this afternoon, their mother would, in all likelihood, never meet the babies that emerged. So why fight? What was there to fight about?

In the warm sunlight, Sam said, "You know, I bet we will have our kids here." Her mother smiled at her, and Sam smiled back. Nestled in the place her mother did not perceive was Sam's real future: the funeral, the sale, the final ferry out.

Sam had told herself she didn't grasp what made her sister, their mother, and their mother's mother act the way they did. That wasn't true, though, was it? She felt it at work in her core. Sam would take pain—the lie told, the self stifled—as long as she got one pleasurable moment out of it. She'd slog for ten years in food service to preserve a single well-loved vision. She'd keep herself apart from new relationships; she'd betray their dying mother's wishes; she'd nod along with Elena's convictions that they should sink their hands into the gold-tipped fur of a bear. All of that was worth it, if, in the end, Sam and her sister got safely out of here.

Their grandmother, in a knee-length skirt, pedaling her bicycle. Their mother wrapping her arms around the two-faced man she must have adored. Sam sharing a pillow with her mother while they watched soap operas. Elena calling—*hello?*—across the trees. It didn't matter if it hurt. They did what they had to. They took their joys where they could find them, because they knew, every one of them, that joys were few and far between. Sam would embrace it, this moment, drinking coffee in the sun with her mother. Short and false as it was—who cared? This was the way her family sustained itself. This was how they would last.

WHEN SAM DISEMBARKED IN FRIDAY HARBOR THE next afternoon, Ben was waiting on the dock. "What took you so long?" he asked. His hair was curling from the damp breeze. It always took her a while to leave after her shift was done; she had to wipe everything down, close out the register, and do a last sweep through the dining area for trash. He, meanwhile, strolled off, unencumbered, and had time to smoke a cigarette.

She took one from him. The lighter, too. "I didn't know you were getting off this early."

"I worked a double yesterday," he said. "Feel like lunch?"

"I can't."

"Ah." He squinted at the water. The ferry, behind Sam, blasted its horn twice. On the dock around them, people were strapping their kids into strollers and their dogs into complicated chest harnesses. He had waited for her, she guessed, because he wanted to sleep together; he'd disembarked in Friday Harbor a couple times before, under the pretense of taking Sam for a date at a restaurant in town. In each instance she had redirected him to her car's backseat,

where they could unzip themselves quickly enough for him
to make the next boat out. He said, "You're busy, huh?
Packed schedule? You've got to go right now?"

"Yeah. I am. You should've found me on board."

"I came by. You were on your phone all day."

She'd been looking up the hours of outdoor outfitters.
"Well," she said. "Anyway. I do have to go."

"What's so important?"

"I have to run an errand, and then—you know. My
mom."

"Oh, yeah," Ben said. "Sorry." He knit his brows. The
thick black fringe of his lashes framed his eyes, honey
brown, with darkness. "What's the errand? Want help?"

"You don't need to."

"But I want to," he said.

Sam squinted at him. Wanted to, why?

The dock was almost emptied out. A single terminal at-
tendant was picking up litter from the holding area. Sam
ground her cigarette under her foot. Ben reached for her
bag and she, after a moment, gave it to him to carry. He
asked, "Where're we headed?"

The "we" sounded off. In one instant, Ben could be silly,
stupid, making fun, and then in the next he would unsettle
her by asking her to meals. Texting on the days their shifts
didn't overlap. At times he acted almost like a boyfriend. He
didn't need to bother; Sam had enough to deal with.

"Kings Marine," Sam said. "I've got to get something."

Kings Marine didn't have it. Its second floor was narrowly geared toward boaters, with crab traps and fishing guides and waterproof electronics for sale. Ben wandered across the floor, fingering buoys and woven black nets. "What are we looking for?" he asked.

"Bear spray."

His palms stopped on a life jacket. "Really? What happened, it came back?"

"That biologist told me to get some," Sam said. "In case."

"I thought you didn't trust her."

When had Sam told him that? Sitting in the galley, tucked into crew quarters, waiting alongside him for the boat to dock—there had been too many opportunities for Sam to chatter. "I didn't say that."

Ben moved over to a barrel full of kayak paddles. "Sure."

Sam was standing in front of a shelf of insect repellents. She picked up a can and put it back down. "She's just super weird," she said. "Holier than thou."

"I get it. She makes you insecure."

Sam turned away from the cans and toward him. He was smiling at her, he thought they were bantering, but her skin was hot. She said, "Fuck off."

"Whoa. Feeling sensitive?"

"No, I'm great," Sam said. "I'm fantastic. I just think it's funny that you're defending this person when she would never—she's so out of your league."

Because she was facing him, she saw the words land. He'd hurt her accidentally, but she in turn had tried to hurt him, and it worked: his smile dropped off. A wound opened.

Ben turned from her. After a second of silence, he walked away. Sam faced the row of repellents and picked up another can as if the mosquito illustration on it would transform into a bear.

Her eyes burned. She almost felt as though she ought to apologize, but—he owed *her* an apology, she thought—any hurt here was his fault. Wasn't it?

Sure, there were qualities in Madeline that . . . did unsettle Sam, made her regret every interaction, told her to keep the biologist away. Madeline could not have made it more clear with the way she looked and wrote and carried herself that she and Sam were from different worlds. Sam shouldn't trust her.

Except that was what confused Sam most. As foreign as Madeline's life must be, she was also potentially recognizable . . . It didn't make sense. Ben could never understand; Sam herself didn't. But Madeline and Elena both made Sam want to follow their leadership. When Madeline gave directions, Sam was tempted, against her older sister's guidance, to obey. That was the part that unnerved Sam, and intrigued her, and made her think about the biologist and write desperate emails and talk about her, apparently, too much.

Someone touched her back and she started. The cans clattered against each other. Ben was next to her, his hand lifted. He said, "Hey. I talked to a person who works here and they've got nothing. Let's try somewhere else."

They walked five minutes down Spring Street to the
hardware store. At the entrance, Ben again put his fingers
on Sam's back. Small points of warmth—five dots of accu-
sation. Low, Sam said to him, "It's not what you think. I'm
fine with her. It's just best to not, you know, get close to
what's too different."

"Right," he said. "That's why you won't with me."

"I don't—"

"Because I intimidate you with my beauty," he said.
Winked at her. Those lush dark lashes, that relaxed and too-
clever look.

She didn't say anything else, and neither did he. They
looked down separate aisles, came up empty, and recon-
vened at the help desk, where a man in a red apron offered
to special-order Sam a canister. "So you've seen our bear?"
he asked.

Sam nodded. Ben spoke up: "Right outside her house."

"My goodness," the man said. "It's really getting bold.
Do you know the Gerards? They saw it last week around
their property, and now their outdoor cats are missing."

"Shit," Ben said. "That's awful."

The man shook his head. He was typing something on
his computer. "Anyway, you're not the first people to come
in asking about this. Can never be too careful." He hit a
key. "The spray'll be here in a week. It'll run you fifty-five
bucks—fifty-four ninety-five, technically."

He might as well have said a year and a thousand dollars.
An eternity and a sack of precious stones. This was time and

money Sam did not have. Ben had moved a few feet away, to the side of the desk, to toy with a display rack of fishing lures. In his hands, the feathers and hooks.

She said, "Can I ask you a favor?"

"Sure," Ben said. "Shoot."

"Can I borrow fifty-five dollars? For ordering this thing? And then I'd pay you back next Friday?"

He pulled away from the lures. The make-believe, for a moment, dropped, and Ben showed himself to Sam as he really was: reluctant. His pretty mouth was tight. Despite all his invitations, he wasn't her boyfriend at all, was he? Just an island visitor, a guy who came to San Juan for the season and fucked her.

He'd gotten off the boat today to rub that in her face. Ben assumed she was ignorant because he had lived a bigger life than she had. He'd grown up elsewhere, served in the Coast Guard Reserve, traveled. What had Sam learned from these years at home, meanwhile? What lessons did she have to carry with her? All she knew was exactly what she'd tried to tell him: never, ever turn to a stranger for help.

"Never mind," Sam said.

"No, I—" He hesitated. "Sam, you just . . . How much?"

"Forget it."

Ben's usual face was back on. He reached as if to touch his wallet but didn't actually go into his pocket. His arm hovered there. "If you really need it," he said, "it's no prob-lem."

"No," she said. "I'm good." His hand fell to his side. He

was controlling himself now, but he was relieved. Sam knew. She pulled out her phone, both to check the time and to look away from him. "It's late."

Ben followed her out of the store, up Spring Street, toward the harbor where her car was parked. She stayed a step ahead so he couldn't touch her anymore. He was talking about another deckhand. Some argument they'd gotten into, the funny things Ben had said in response. Sam was thinking about fifty-five dollars: two twenties, a ten, and a five. Only a few bills, and yet more than she had, more than he thought she was worth.

His family was better off than hers was. It was obvious. He'd gone to two years of college but never talked about student loans. He wore Red Wing boots, name-brand, nice stuff, and had a newer cellphone. His parents were together. They were retired, he'd told Sam, during one of his talks with her before or after sex, in the bantering runup or the soft comedown.

Sam's mother would never get to retire. Even if she hadn't gotten sick—she would have never been able to afford it. The sisters themselves needed a human sacrifice in order to stop working even for a short while. Yet Ben, strolling beside her, carrying her bag, had everything. Fifty-five dollars a hundred times over, probably. More. He was playing, during the pandemic, at working life; he occupied the job Sam hadn't been offered and a place on the boat where she'd been kept from shifts; he acted like he knew her reality, but he had no idea. What Sam had been through. How much four bills might change.

They reached the parking lot. At its edge stood an art installation Sam had walked past ten thousand times before: a carved wooden post showing a woman embracing a mountain lion. Sam needed to get off this island already. Interrupting Ben's telling of a story he'd heard about the first mate, she said, "Bye."

He halted, regrouped. "You're sure you don't have time for a meal?" She shook her head. "Do you have a couple minutes, even? We could just hang."

Ah. Right. He would give her nothing when she needed it, but now that he'd walked eight blocks round-trip with her, he could get what he wanted in the first place. The backseat, the locked doors, the fumbled clothes. "No," she said. "I don't."

He pouted, fleetingly. "What's your shift tomorrow?"

"Morning. Five."

"I'm not on until two."

"Okay," she said. She didn't care. She was over it: Ben's body, his talking, his thrusting, his jokes. Their connection to each other had run its short course.

She unlocked her car. Ben was lingering. He asked, "Are you all right?"

"Sure."

He tipped his head at her.

She couldn't help herself. What he had to say didn't matter anymore, but still. "Why do you even have this job?" she asked.

"What does that mean?"

"Why? You have a degree. Isn't there something better you should do?"

"What, cure cancer? I like being on the water," he said. Sam shook her head. He protested: "So? What's wrong with that?"

"Nothing. I didn't say anything."

"Okay, except you're pissed off, it's obvious."

"I'm not," she said. "Like what you like. Who cares? I'm fine."

"Come on," Ben said. The sun was high and the breeze was blowing off the water. She could see every individual hair in the stubble on his cheeks. The peach fuzz on his earlobes. Looking at him made her remember the closets they'd hid themselves in, his face too close to focus on, his fingers deep inside. His voice so different there from what it sounded like out here, with the tourists passing and the gulls calling behind. "This is about the money?"

"No."

"I can lend it to you if you need it. I told you that."

"I just think it's shitty that you have this job," Sam said, "when you could do something else. Whatever. You're always talking about going back to school. Why don't you do that? Because there are people here who could really use what you have. People who don't have a lot of other options."

"The job was open and I applied," he said. "If they wanted it, they should've applied, too."

Sam found this infuriating. The car door handle was warming under her hand. How casual he was, how wrong. "You think I'm stupid," she said. "You're the stupid one."

He made a face. "I don't think that at all. You need to calm down."

"Don't tell me that."

"You're overreacting. You're this pissed because we—"

"It's not about the money," Sam said. And it wasn't. It was but it wasn't—it wasn't about *this* money, these particular fifty-five dollars, but about all the money, his parents' imagined money, the money in this country that was kept away from her family, the money in the pockets of the passengers they ferried back and forth. All the things other people had. And she had nothing. She had less than that.

It wasn't fair that Ben should move around, rent his own place, go fishing when he felt like it. It enraged her. His total lack of appreciation for what he had. It wasn't about the money; it was about him, and her, and where they came from, and the whole world, which was twisted and threatening and completely unfair, which demanded that Sam defend herself but never gave her any of what she needed to try.

"Forget it," she said. "Seriously. We've wasted enough time together. I've got to get back home."

THEIR HOUSE SIMMERED. WHEN SHE GOT BACK, SAM ate the leftovers in the fridge, and then Elena, after work, berated her about the dirty dishes. Their mother that evening was agitated, calling out about discomfort. She made noises for them from down the hall. Elena gripped the sides of the sink and said to Sam, "Can you take care of it?" The *for once?* wasn't said but was implied. Elena wanted to be left alone in the kitchen to fantasize about her bear lover. Sam slammed her chair against the edge of the table when she stood. Once she got to the bedroom, she found her mother had pushed her blanket back and was complaining about dizziness. Her mother said her chest hurt. She wanted to call the doctor. Sam had to promise her they would. It took Sam a long time to settle her mother, smooth the bedding over her swollen legs and abdomen, find a good television show, turn up the oxygen, and assure her that everything would be all right.

By the time Sam got back to the kitchen, the lights were out. Elena wasn't in the living room. Sam turned uselessly

around the house looking for her sister before being forced
to give her a call. Elena picked up after one ring: "I'm taking a walk."

Sam's jaw tightened. "Where?"

"Outside."

"Are you . . ." Sam didn't know how to put it. The bear,
the bear. "Do you expect to see something out there?
Or . . ."

Elena laughed, a short blast of breath. "Sammy. Chill
out. I'm walking, that's all. I'll be back soon."

Sam hung up. Thought of calling back—should she ask
to join? Sam would love to tell Elena about Ben. And if the
bear came, Sam could protect her . . . She remembered,
then, that she had nothing to protect her sister with. She
was sprayless, empty-handed. Sam hated being in this house
but had no options outside it. She wiped the kitchen count-
ers and went to her room to lie down.

Elena must've returned after Sam fell asleep. Sam, who
had to leave for work the next morning while it was still
dark, looked behind the curtain in the living room before
she went. Her sister lay at peace. During Sam's shift, Elena
texted a few times: their mother was still worked up; Elena
had left a message for the doctor; their mother had vom-
ited; her breathing didn't sound good. Sam tucked her
phone under the register. It went silent between islands,
then buzzed when they were coming into port.

Sam's shoulders hurt. Her muscles were sore from tension. Rich ladies who had this kind of ache, she knew, got hour-long massages, but Sam only climbed into her car after her shift ended and drove home.

She let herself into a quiet house. Checking the bedroom, she saw her mother was sleeping. Sam perched on the side of the bed, careful not to rock her, and watched. The skin under her mother's eyes was dark. A bruise. Her face was thin. She was the bedrock of Sam's small world.

When Sam and Elena were children, their mother used to take them on temperate evenings to play by the fairgrounds. She sat at a picnic table while they occupied themselves on the swings. She wore sunglasses. She could've been their big sister. If they asked, she'd push them, her hands firm and flat against their backs. She made them more powerful every time she touched them. They soared up, away from the wood chips on the ground, toward the wide sky and the lowering circle of the sun.

The room smelled stale and sour. They should leave the door open to let it air out.

Their doorbell rang. Sam started, making the mattress move, so her mother was jostled but did not, thank God, wake up. Sam stood and hurried to the front. Someone was knocking.

She opened the door to, of all people, Madeline Pettit, in her work clothes and without a single flyaway hair. "Sam," Madeline said. "Glad I caught you. I called today but didn't hear back."

"Oh," Sam said. "Today was busy—I—" There was no

explanation. She hadn't anticipated ever seeing Madeline in person again. Madeline's arrival didn't mean Sam was breaking her promise to Elena, did it? "Did we make plans or—?"

"No. I had to be in San Juan to meet with a few folks and thought it might be a good opportunity to bring you this." Madeline swung her bag forward, pulled out a plastic-wrapped canister, and presented it to Sam. A red cap. Bear spray.

"Oh," Sam said again. Out on the road, a car passed. Dumb, Sam added, "They're expensive."

Madeline's cool expression didn't shift. "We have them at the office. After we emailed, I figured I would bring one your way."

Sam took the canister in both hands. Its plastic was slick under her fingers. Having spent the last day heated with anger, she couldn't quite arrange herself into someone who could make sense of this gift—she still felt warm and frustrated, but those feelings had no clear direction now. "Thanks."

Madeline shrugged. "The spray can be comforting simply to carry. While the bear doesn't pose a threat, I can understand why you and your neighbors might have concerns about his presence. I don't know if you've heard, but he was spotted over the weekend on the northwest coast. It's possible that he's swum on by now."

"Right," Sam said. "No, I didn't know that. Great." She and Elena had walked up to it in the woods on Friday—could it be gone that easily? She stared at the can so Madeline couldn't read her face. "Thanks again."

"Not a problem. Have you or your sister had any more sightings?"

Sam didn't hesitate. "No."

"Good," Madeline said. There was nothing more to say, but Madeline kept standing there. After a long moment, she spoke again: "I've been thinking about your message. The idea of the bear approaching you. That would be very unusual. An escalation in nuisance behavior, which is exactly what we're trying to avoid."

The swirl in Sam's body continued. "Uh-huh."

"It could happen, though, if someone has been luring him, either unintentionally or not. Bears used to humans lose their usual wariness. Have you heard of anyone doing such a thing?"

Sam shook her head. "No." She couldn't look up.

Madeline paused. Sam could hear, in that silence, a wish that Sam would rush into talk. Confess. She wasn't going to. Finally, Madeline said, "Glad to hear it. Doing so can not only be dangerous for the animal, but also result in legal consequences for the people involved."

The plastic wrapping the canister was marked with a dotted line, showing where to peel it open. Madeline's boots stood firm on the front walk. Her laces were crusted with dried mud. Inside Sam, the truth—the animal, her sister, their meeting, the risk—hummed. "Cool," Sam said. "Okay, well, thank you again, Madeline, we appreciate it. Have a good day." She backed up and shut the door.

For the next four hours, Sam sat on the sofa in the living

room, completed quizzes, and sweated. What did Madeline suspect? What had she heard? Elena's walk to and from work took her along the edges of dozens of private properties. Had someone seen Elena on the trail dropping breadcrumbs and calling for the bear to come near?

Madeline had made her words sound like a threat. "Legal consequences." But she had coupled those words with a gift . . . Sam couldn't sort it out. She reached the end of one survey and began another. She was getting close again to the website's threshold for cashing out. Her mother made a sound from the back room, and Sam went to check.

At last the time crept toward six o'clock, when Elena would be near. Sam couldn't wait any longer. She put her sneakers on, tucked the can of bear spray into her back pocket, and headed out the door. The sun was getting lower in the sky but the road was still warm from the day's heat. Sam stared down the pavement, praying for Elena to appear.

And then: there she was. Elena coming dreamily around the corner. Her polo, neat on her shoulders, exposed her long, thin arms. Her bag hung over one side. Raising a hand, Sam called, "El!" Her sister came to attention and waved.

Sam hurried to meet her. She was already past the Larsens' property. She wanted to tell Elena about Madeline's visit, the free can, the warning given. That their mother was having another bad day. How much oxygen she'd needed to use. Together, they'd walk to the house, where Elena would make them pasta for dinner. Birds called from the treetops along the road. Elena drifted to the pavement's edge, and Sam saw, in the space her sister had vacated, a gliding movement in the woods.

Sam froze. Elena kept walking. Whatever was behind her stopped—had Sam . . . ?—she stared. No. No, there it was, moving again. Alive.

Only a couple hundred feet behind Elena, and coming steadily forward. Flashes of brown behind lines of bark. Sam should not shout, it could be too dangerous, but she had to warn her sister. She held up both hands, fingers spread, to give warning. She pointed. Jabbed into the air. They might be too far from each other for Elena to read Sam's lips, but Sam mouthed the word anyway. Breathed it: *Bear.*

Elena nodded. She didn't change her pace.

Sam's adrenaline was spiking. The muscles in her thighs seized. Out in the forest on Friday, when she and Elena met it, Sam had only barely been kept in place by shock and her sister's surety and the overwhelming dread of being attacked if she faced away, but now, here, knowing what she needed to do was actually march toward it, she was paralyzed. She couldn't. For a moment, in the woods, there was nothing, and then—there it was again. Its body appeared and vanished. It was walking the fine line between their human existence and monstrosity. She didn't know how quickly it could move.

She had to help Elena. She had to. She tried to talk but

her vocal cords were locked. Finally, she got some sound out—shouted. "Hurry."

Elena was getting close. Amusement played over her face. "It's all right," she called to Sam.

Elena was calling backwards, too, Sam knew. Using this easygoing voice to calm them all.

The bear's full body wasn't yet visible, but Sam knew it anyway, knew it too well. How massive it was. Its claws and teeth—its appetites.

Elena continued her easy talk. "Our friend followed me home. I gave him some leftover roast beef from the club and he couldn't get enough, I guess." As near as she was, Sam could see the shine in Elena's eyes, a glow like a girl bewitched. Elena had walked two miles home with this predator at her back, and she was speaking as though behind her was nothing more vicious than a pine squirrel. It wasn't possible. It wasn't right. Sam had pushed away Madeline's questions in favor of Elena's good judgment . . .

And then, mercifully, Sam remembered: the spray. The idea of it allowed her body to loosen. She pulled it from her back pocket, a cold can, and fumbled with the top. They had seconds, maybe, only, if the bear started to run. Elena was saying something else—what—but Sam wasn't listening. She worked against the clip-on top. She couldn't figure it out. The trigger pulled.

The hiss. The cloud. A burst under her finger, a line in the sky.

THEY HAD TO FLUSH OUT THEIR EYES AND MOUTHS with water afterward. Together, they hunched over the kitchen sink. From the back of the house came nothing but silence, and Sam had to be grateful for that, because if their mother had asked what happened, there could be no explanation. Sam's throat was scraped raw by capsaicin. Even her clothing burned. The water was cold but it did not do enough.

Elena, at Sam's side, was a blur, a fuzzy figure bent with disapproval. She wasn't pretending to speak happily anymore. Over the sound of the rushing sink: "What the hell."

Sam pressed her wet hands to her cheeks. She had to force words out past raw peppered flesh. "Bear spray."

Elena didn't respond. It took fifteen long minutes of washing before Sam's vision mostly returned, and with it, the sight of her sister, eyelashes clumped, hair dripping, complexion swollen and flared red. They both had to change out their clothes for items that weren't contaminated. Elena carried everything to the washing machine.

Down the hall, doors opened and shut. Sam wanted to peel her skin off, too, finish the job that the spray had started.

Elena came back and picked up the emptied can on the counter. She squinted at it. " 'Use to deter attacking animals,' " she read. "Were we being attacked?"

"It was right there."

Elena kept reading. " 'Range of up to forty feet.' Really, Sammy?"

Sam's body was on fire.

"Did you even look at the directions before you used this thing?"

"I'm not a little kid," Sam said. "You don't need to talk to me that way."

Elena put the can down. "That's funny. You sure do act like it."

Sam sucked air in. It tingled, ice crystals, on the insides of her scorched cheeks. "I do? When you— Elena, you're out offering roast beef to bears. I am trying to help us—"

"Oh my gosh, thank you." Elena syrupy with sarcasm. Her eyes rimmed red.

"You're totally—you've lost track of what we're supposed to be doing. You're in the woods pretending you're the spirit of San Juan. But you're not. Okay? You're not. Sorry to break it to you."

Elena's mouth got tight.

Sam kept going. She still burned. She didn't know exactly what she was saying but she knew she needed to make

Elena make sense again. "I get that you're worn out, and it's been . . . an exciting distraction for you, or whatever, but enough is enough, we have to . . ."

Elena picked up the can again. "How much did this cost?"

Sam stopped. "Madeline gave it to me."

"Who?"

"The biologist. From the state. She came by with it today."

Elena turned from Sam. Her shoulders bowed forward. The back of her neck was pale, a long stretch of fine bone. She was holding the can in front of herself where Sam couldn't see. The loneliness of that body, faced away, was devastating.

"Where are the car keys?" Elena said. When Sam asked why, what for, Elena said she was going to sleep at Kristine's.

"You can't," Sam said. "Mom's not doing well. She needs you."

Elena said she'd come back in a few hours, then, but she was going. She put the can down. Its metal rim clinked on the counter. A hollow noise. Sam trailed after her to the hall, where Elena dug out the car keys from Sam's bag. They jingled in Elena's palm. Sam knew exactly how her sister felt, the pepper spread across her skin, the flames licking her eyes and nostrils, the burn in her hair follicles; she understood the urge to run away, she felt it all the time. Stay here, she told Elena. Don't go out there. Stay. Elena left.

SAM ATE BY HERSELF THAT EVENING. SHE'D BURIED THE used bear spray can in the garbage while her food heated. Black-sided, red-topped: she couldn't stand to look at it. Elena was out there, wandering without her, because of that thing. In the back bedroom, their mother was fitful, in and out of sleep. The muscles in her cheeks were drawn tight by pain. Sam washed her plate and utensils in the sink. She watched the window.

Hours passed that way. Dusk was coming. Sam texted Elena, but got no response. When, at last, a person moved on the road, Sam tugged her shoes on and went outside. It was only Danny Larsen walking his dog, but still, it was someone.

Danny watched as she came down the front walk. His smile, that constant mask, was mediated. Tender. He looked almost worried for her. "How are you doing?" he called.

"Did you see it today?" Sam asked.

He hesitated. "See what?"

"The bear was right on our road. A couple hours ago. You didn't see?" Sam pointed down the pavement.

Danny turned to look after. The dog bounded around his knees. Before this month, the only times Sam and Danny had stood so close were accidents, bumping into each other while she ran an errand in the pharmacy or brushing by on the way to class. He was still big, he carried muscle, but time and his beard had softened him. At this distance, Sam could see how landscaping had aged his skin.

"No way," he said. "Right there?"

"You really didn't see it?" Sam let her arm drop. "Doesn't it . . . It's never come onto your property?" Was her family really the only one pursued?

"Not that we know of. But we've got the dog." Danny leaned to rub its yellow back for emphasis. His fingers played in its fur. The dog lifted its head, stretching its long throat, and grinned. Its lips were black and teeth brushed white. "She barks at everything that moves out the window. Wildlife stays away."

"Well, hooray for you," Sam said. She sounded nastier than she had to, she knew.

Danny didn't slip toward irritation. If anything, the wrinkles between his eyebrows deepened. "Want to keep her at your place for a bit?"

"Oh," Sam said. Automatically: "No, no."

"She's friendly."

"No," Sam said, "it's— No. Thanks. It'd be too much for my mom, I think. Any barking." She felt flushed. Couldn't tell if it was discomfort from Danny always being so nice or the lingering pepper spray.

"How is your mom?"

"She's okay."

Danny was studying her. Asking in silence for more. To her surprise, then, she gave it to him. "She's not great. It's been a tough few days."

"I'm sorry to hear that."

Sam shook her head. Against her better judgment, she liked his sympathy—liked talking to someone, anyone, after these hours solo in the house. Liked being treated gently. Her face and neck stayed warm.

"The offer for the dog stands," he said. "And I'd be glad to help with whatever else you all might need."

"More home repairs."

"Sure," he said. "Hammer at the ready over here."

Sam laughed, a little, in spite of herself. "Well," she said. "Thanks. If one of our windows jams, I know who to call."

"Do. I'm serious." His eyes were clear, steady blue. The quiet sea. "Do you have my number?"

Sam stuttered at that. No, she— Why would she? He didn't blink. He had her take out her phone. He recited the digits while she punched them in, and saved them, and there it was: Danny Larsen in her contact list.

"Text me so I have yours," he said, and she did.

Her phone showed no notifications. Elena hadn't written back. Sam returned it to her pocket to wait. The dog, tongue out, was curled at Danny's feet.

"What would you do if you did see the bear?" Sam asked.

"I don't know. Take a picture? It's pretty special to see, right?"

Its thick, rippling, brutal arms as it stepped forward, shifting its weight from side to side. Elena's monstrous shadow. "I'm not sure about special," Sam said.

He shrugged. "That's just what I heard."

The last time, he told her he'd run for his gun. "You wouldn't shoot it?" she asked.

"Whoa," Danny said. His beard curled over his chin and hid the corners of his mouth, so she couldn't tell what quirks were there, the edges that would expose whether he thought she was ridiculous. She could only see his furrowed brows. Those deep blue eyes. "I don't even know if that's legal."

"But if it was a danger to you?"

"Is that what's going on?" he asked. "Are you all right?"

Sam couldn't answer. The bear hadn't harmed Elena, but it kept coming closer to her, sniffing around her body, seeking to be soothed by her hands. How long would it be before it bit down? And even if it never touched them, Sam felt the risk it ran her family. Everything about the bear was dangerous.

She didn't know how to convey this to someone who was, at best, a neighbor, and who was really only a stranger. She said, "We're fine."

He chewed on his cheek. Up close, his face was sweeter, both older and younger, than Sam had expected. "I get that you're scared," he said. "It's a scary situation."

Sam had to nod at that. "Elena walks to work every day."

He sighed. "I know." He had seen her, then, moving pale and graceful down their road, vanishing onto the trail where a bear prowled. He had liked Elena once; he noticed her still. How could he not? That beauty. The princess of Portland Fair Road.

"It could come near—"

"Sam," he said, "you know, we can't make people do what they don't want to do. If that's what she's decided, then you've got to accept it."

"Yeah," Sam said. "No. I know that."

He opened his mouth to say more, then stopped. "I mean," he said. "You should ask her to be careful, definitely. If you want. But you can't . . ."

Sam said, "Wouldn't you be worried about her, too, if you were me?"

She was seeking, for reasons she couldn't quite sort, Danny's continued tenderness, his low and gentle voice. She got it. The sound washed over her. Cool tap water across burning skin. "No doubt I would be," he said. "Absolutely. Sam, I get— I see how important you are to each other. How close you are."

And it was probably just her loneliness, Elena's absence, the breakup with Ben, the stress of her mother, but hearing that made tears come to Sam's eyes. Prickling there, welling at her lash lines. She couldn't look at Danny anymore. She stared at the dog instead. Dumb thing, with its tongue hanging.

Danny kept going. "Elena knows what she's doing," he said. "She's so smart. You can trust her, Sam, I promise. This is going to be okay." God, the sound of him. His solidness. When she stood here, beside him, she didn't feel that any bear would dare step out of the falling darkness. He and the dog seemed to come from a different plane of existence, where life went along easy and nothing hurt. This close to him, Sam could enter that world, too, almost. It felt unbearably good. It made her cry.

SAM WOKE THAT NIGHT TO HER SISTER IN HER BEDROOM. The space was black. It had to be before three-thirty—Sam's alarm hadn't yet gone off—what time was it?—late, late. Elena's hand gripped her shoulder, and her face was close, her breath warm. Her hair caught the barest light from the window so loose strands of it looked white as stars.

"Sammy," Elena whispered. And Sam knew. There could be no other reason for this. "You need to wake up. Mom's gone."

THEY HAD PREPARED FOR THIS MOMENT HALF THEIR lives, the sisters, but Sam followed Elena to their mother's bedroom in disbelief. The light was on in there. The brightness was obscene. Elena moved without any hesitation but Sam had to squint against it. She was afraid to look and see—their mother. Their mother. Their mother had been alive only a few hours earlier; Sam had brought her to the bathroom, held her hands, given her water, tucked the sheets around her in bed and told her she'd see her when she woke up.

Now here their mother was. In that same bed, but transformed. Her cheeks weren't held tight anymore. Her mouth hung open.

Elena was at her bedside. Her back was to Sam. "I just came in to check and found her."

Sam nodded.

In the room was only the sound of their breath. The sisters. The television wasn't on and neither was their mother's oxygen. Sam couldn't tell what exact time it was. Her phone was in the other room, next to the bed. Should she get it?

Sam asked, "Did you?" Elena was silent. That didn't make sense, Sam realized, what she'd said. She tried again. "We should call 911?"

Elena said, "She's cold."

Sam needed to put the blanket on her. She stepped forward.

Then she understood what Elena meant: their mother's body. They were past resuscitation. It was done.

Sam sat down on the floor. Her knees simply released. She fell cross-legged and her ankles hit hard on the ground. The pain was sudden, a shot, then faded. She and Elena used to sit like this, crisscross applesauce, in classrooms, at their teachers' direction. They were kids. Their mother was so young then. Glamorous. She hadn't gotten sick yet. When it was their birthdays, she surprised them at school with grocery-store mini cupcakes. Twelve to a pack. Sam remembered the icing on those: perfect. Machine-made spirals of chocolate and vanilla with purple circular sprinkles on top that tasted like chalk. Their mother stood by the whiteboard and beamed while everyone sang "Happy Birthday." She must've had to take off work for those afternoons. She never minded.

When had their mother stopped doing that? In what grade? Sam couldn't remember. She should ask Elena. Later.

Sitting, Sam was at the level of the bed. She was face-to-face with her mother, who was pale, Sam could see now, bleached-looking, like the logs that washed up on the shore. Sam could smell the sheets. Dried sweat. Should be laundered. Her mother's ear was very fine, the whorl of it, a seashell. Her jaw was soft. Slack. Her lips were dry. Those lovely top teeth, white and shining, were exposed. They'd been put in her gums when she was a teen, and they'd outlasted her, outlasted her heart and lungs and living soul.

Elena was crying. Her hip, next to Sam, shook. Her whole body was shaking. Voice warped by tears, she said, "Didn't you hear anything?"

"Hear what?"

"From Mom? Before?"

"I didn't," Sam said. It wasn't clear to her what she was supposed to say. What Elena wanted. "I was asleep."

Elena was gasping. She should be crying, too, Sam thought of herself—well, she'd cry soon. When someone died, people cried. That's what happened. Their mother had cried for years about their grandmother. Her nose got pink on the end like a bunny's. How adorable she was. No wonder men had been drawn to her. Their mother loved them all so much. Their mother.

What were they going to do without their mother? Her stories? Her care? Every day would be empty.

The room was too quiet. Sam wouldn't have to go to the pharmacy as much, she thought. Or the doctor's office anymore. They ought to call him, Dr. Boyce, and tell him. What time was it? They should leave a message. Or was it too early, too late?

Elena swallowed. Some great wet lump was in her throat. Sam was dry-faced, like their mother, who lay there in front of them, relieved of the need to fight. Sam wanted to touch her. She did touch her. Sam's hand, she was surprised to observe, trembled. She put her fingers on her mother's shoulder, like Elena had touched Sam's shoulder, only minutes before, in the other bedroom, to wake her. When Sam was sleeping and didn't yet know. Sam said, "Mom?"

Elena was right. Their mother's warmth had vanished. She was room temperature: cool and dry and gone.

Elena kept sobbing. The sound of it—saturated. She said, "We should've been with her. She was alone. She shouldn't have been alone."

AFTER, THERE WERE SO MANY THINGS TO DO. SAM AND Elena called out of work. They sat on the living room sofa while Elena phoned the funeral home. People came to pick up the body. It seemed Elena and their mother had discussed all this: how many copies of the death certificate the family would need, how to arrange for direct cremation. Elena read a credit card number into the phone while Sam stared after.

Elena took care of everything. She spread out papers on the kitchen table—their mother's bank statements, the car and house titles—and made more calls. The cell service, internet, and utilities were in their mother's name. Elena brought out their mother's tax returns. She called the probate court and waited on hold, tears running down her cheeks.

Sam stripped their mother's bed. She took the last glass their mother had used to the sink, where she scrubbed, rinsed, rubbed it dry with a cloth. The house still smelled of their mother. Her shampoo, her breath. The bedroom held her emptied oxygen tanks. Sam sat in there and watched an episode of a soap.

Sam had imagined their mother's passing as a release from long disease, a bitter kind of liberation. But now she just wanted her mom back. Having her mother was natural. It was foundational. Sam was hollowed, while at the front of the house, Elena wept on.

The sisters slept in their mother's bed each night. Time passed too slowly and too fast.

On Wednesday, Elena went back to work. Sam said she should stay home longer, but Elena shook her head. Sam drove her over to the club. Returning to the empty house was awful. Sam crawled into their mother's bed to nap. When she went out again, early that evening, to pick Elena up, she found a casserole dish on the front step. Its tinfoil cover had been ripped open and the lasagna it once contained eaten out. Tomato sauce smeared the concrete.

The bear. Its presence, at their home, in this moment, was offensive. An insult. That it should come here, now, and take more from them, when in these past few days they'd already lost so much.

Sam picked up the dish and brought it inside to scrape what was left into the trash can. Washing it, she found herself shivering. There was no note. The bear took the note? Did it do these things on purpose, did it intuit what would hurt them most? Or did it operate on instinct in order to ruin their lives? If it came next into their home, shat on top of their mother's bedding, she wouldn't be surprised. God—she hated the thing. Its proximity. Its behavior. She tucked the rinsed casserole dish into a cupboard and went out to the car to get Elena.

She didn't tell Elena about the bear's red-stained visit. She wanted it and her sister to stay as distant as possible. Elena, meanwhile, announced that she'd arranged with the club to hold a gathering in their mother's memory that Saturday. Sam asked, "Why? Who's going to come?"

"Mom's friends," Elena said. "Our friends."

"What friends?"

Elena shook her head. "Neighbors. People she used to work with. People we know."

Sam didn't see the point. She told Elena she thought it was stupid, and Elena said she didn't care what Sam thought, their mother would've liked it, and Sam said, no, she wouldn't have, and Elena went into the bathroom and slammed the door. Sam could hear her crying in the shower. All that water doubled up. In her room, Sam tried filling out a survey, but the page reloaded in the middle and she lost the whole thing. She put the phone down next to her and shut her eyes.

The phone buzzed. She picked it up. A text from Ben: *I heard about your mom. So sorry, Sam. Here for you*

She put the phone back down.

Going to bed side by side on their mother's mattress was a return to Elena and Sam's childhood, when they shared a room and let each other's night noises soothe them into sleep. Elena's teeth rubbed together when she dreamed. Sam took solace from the grind. A third of their household had dropped away; so many of the tiny beloved disruptions that Sam had come to rely on—their mother's door opening, the rise of her voice, the background chatter from her television—were absent. Sam needed Elena now more than ever. Even when they bickered, their sisterhood, the strength of it, held.

FRIDAY DAWNED UNSEASONABLY WARM. AIR SAT STICKY. They went out early to scatter their mother's ashes between the trees deep on their property, where camas flowers bloomed white and purple and delicate hemlock needles whispered overhead. Elena knelt in the dirt to spread the cremains with her fingers. Sam stood behind to watch. Her sister's shoulders shone with sweat already. That was their mother, there, Sam told herself of the gray on the ground, but it was difficult to believe—the transformation from woman, life-giver, to dirt. Her ashes rolled into the earth under Elena's palms. At last Elena stood, her cheeks slick, and said, "We'll get a stone soon. I looked online. Some aren't too expensive."

Back at the house for breakfast, they opened the windows to relieve the heat, but no breeze blew in to help. While Sam, in a tank top, cleared the table, Elena came out in her uniform and said, "When are you going back to work?"

Sam shrugged.

"Today?"

"I don't know," Sam said. She put eggy plates in the sink to soak. "I mean, does it matter?"

Elena blinked. Her pink-rimmed eyes, dressed up for the day by mascara. "Yeah, Sammy, it does. We need the money."

Sam twisted the bag shut on a loaf of bread. "How long before we list the house?"

She'd thought that would be an easy question—one of Elena's many items already checked on her mourning to-do list—but it was met with silence. Then Elena said, "What do you mean?"

The plastic untwisted in Sam's hands. She put the loaf down. "When are we going to list the house for sale? We just have to manage the bills until then, right?"

Elena looked baffled. She hadn't been this disoriented when she woke Sam in the middle of the night to tell her their mother was dead. It was a confusion far too large for this conversation. "We're not going to sell the house."

Sam said, "So we can move."

"We're not—"

"What are you talking about," Sam said, throat tightening. "You told me. Years ago. After you graduated. That this house was worth half a million dollars, and after Mom died, we would sell it, and we would move. You told me that. That's been the plan for a fucking decade."

"I told you that?"

Sam didn't understand. Elena was acting as if this was new. "We literally talk about it all the time."

"No," Elena said, "you talk about moving, yes, I know you want to get out of here, I know that, but I didn't— If I told you that when I was a teenager, then I'm sorry, but I didn't know what I was talking about. We had to remortgage this place, Sam. You have no idea how much debt has piled up from Mom's medical bills. We've been underwater for years. If we sell, only the bank makes money, and we'd have nowhere to live."

Sam heard Elena's words (*I'm sorry*). She heard *remortgage* and *debt piled* but their meaning splintered, mirror fragments, and everything became distorted. Underwater? How? She said, slower, "You told me that we'd sell the house and move off this island. That's what we're going to do." Elena had forgotten, somehow, in her grief. Sam would make her remember.

"You—" Elena went to the table and pulled forward the papers they'd pushed to the corner so they could have their meal. Hot air stirred. "Do you need to see the actual numbers? Have you not noticed the situation we're in? I know you're happy to disappear into your fantasies and leave the tough stuff to me, but didn't they tell you at Dr. Boyce's every time you took Mom in? We owe that office thousands. Plus twelve thousand dollars to the hospital for Mom's emergency room visits last year." She was spreading the papers out. White sheets with black digits and capital letters in lines. "Don't you wonder where your money goes each month? The mortgage payment takes almost everything. The pandemic fucked us. You didn't work for ages. I don't know how we'll ever pay off the credit cards. Just her cremation is costing us eleven hundred. Do you get that? This is it, this is everything. We better make the most of this, because we're not going anywhere."

ON THE DAY OF THEIR MOTHER'S MEMORIAL, SAM WENT back to the boat. The weather was still too hot. The passengers were rude, thoughtless, entitled. She wiped out the microwave after someone complained and processed a return for a coffee someone else had already finished. It didn't matter. Her mother was dead. She and Elena were stuck in that house forever without their mom.

That was what Elena said, anyway. And Sam heard it but couldn't fully absorb it. She'd spent eleven years telling herself the opposite; she would need at least that long to get Elena's newest pronouncement through her head. "Sammy," Elena had said, "we're not going anywhere"—it rang over the sounds of the cash register and the spare change. The boat's engine churned, and through its noise Sam heard Elena say those words again and again and again.

Early in their mother's sickness, Sam and Elena traveled with her on this ferry in order to meet with a specialist. Her diagnosis, at that point, hadn't been clear, and they went over these waters believing they would be greeted on the other side by a handshake, a pill, and a cure. Sam had thought that, anyway. She'd thought that sickness was a stomach bug, the sort of thing that takes a person down for forty-eight hours before they rally. She didn't know how long and lonely disease could be.

Their mother herself must've been well worried to take a family trip to the mainland, but she didn't tell them that; she was still working at the salon at that point, sucking polluted air into her damaged lungs. She acted like her usual self. Elena, Sam believed then, had been optimistic—she'd just started working at the golf club, and during the trip she told them about tourists on the green—but then again maybe she hadn't been. Maybe Elena was already getting ready to mortgage their lives for that appointment and the many more to come. What did Sam know, really, of what had been in Elena's mind? Whether she'd expected at that point for their mother to live one year or fifty? What had Elena and their mother said to each other, what forms were filled out or decisions made, while Sam was watching the widening ripples below?

Because that's what Sam remembered: the water. Her mother sitting at a table on the passenger deck with her head leaning against a plastic windowpane, and the water, dark blue topped with white, rushing by outside. Elena and Sam sat across from her. Elena told another silly story. Their mother's eyes were calm, her eyelids heavy, her forehead smooth. The boat rocked them forward.

Sam was still stuck on the same vessel. Their mother would never see that water again. Sam rang up another customer. Two cups of clam chowder, in this heat. Their mother was gone.

That afternoon, Ben came up to the galley. Sam saw him and glanced away. His body, yellow-vested, stayed in the corner of her vision. He waited for passengers to empty out before he approached the register. "Hi."

"Hey," Sam said. She'd hardly talked all day. The sound of her own voice was a surprise.

He was speaking low and tender. "How are you doing? I've been thinking of you." Before today, he had used this voice with her only in private.

"Grand," she said. "Thanks for checking in."

He didn't bat an eye. Grief put a thicker cushion between Sam and the rest of the world, making it so she couldn't hear anyone outside her head and no one else could hear her. Probably she could scream without him flinching. "I read your mother's obituary online. She sounded like a wonderful person."

Vaguely, Sam remembered: Elena typing something up for the *Journal*. One of Elena's many completed tasks. She had shown it to Sam before submitting, but Sam had only skimmed the text (. . . *survived by her two children* . . .) before handing Elena the phone back. On that screen, their mother turned into nothing but a high school graduation year and a collection of clichés. The obituary flattened her until no sign of her ever having really lived was left.

"She was," Sam said. "She was incredible."

"I wish I'd met her."

Sam twisted up her mouth. "Why?"

Ben's lips, the ones she'd spent this season pressing herself against, parted. She made herself look away. "Because I care about you," he said. "I care about your life."

Sam shook her head.

He pressed on. He had come up here determined, it was clear, to mend things between them. "It mentioned you guys are planning a memorial service?"

"You don't need to do this," Sam said.

She waved forward a waiting customer, and Ben backed away before eventually leaving for a lower deck. That evening, though, crossing the parking lot of the golf club, Sam did wish for the limited comfort of his presence. Elena had been short over texts the whole day. Sam was waiting for the message where Elena apologized and withdrew her declaration about their future, but it hadn't yet appeared. Since their fight, Elena had been taking more showers and walks and time alone, while Sam sat at their kitchen table, avoiding looking at her sister's paperwork and longing for the time when her family had seemed inseparable.

She wanted her sister back. Her mother. Someone.

Elena was standing in front of the club's bar when Sam came in. They hugged each other. They were both in their regular work clothes, but Elena's were more appropriate, Elena's were black. People were milling around. "Mrs. Sheffer is here," Elena said into Sam's ear—their eleventh-grade history teacher. Sam turned to take the place next to Elena, but after a minute, Elena squeezed Sam's arm. "Get a drink if you want one. Help yourself. There's food."

So Sam made herself a plate of pasta salad. She circulated. A good number of their old teachers were there. Their mother's former co-workers, who embraced Sam when they saw her, and who smelled, nostalgically, like solvent. They poured out condolences. Sam listened close but their lungs sounded clear. A few people from the medical center had come, and some of the girls who used to hang around Elena in high school. Elena's co-workers—Kristine, holding a tissue, was talking to the grill's manager, the man who'd fired Sam way back when. Neighbors from their road were there, too. Danny Larsen and his mother. He waved; Sam waved back; she flushed and turned toward the food table.

She heard her mother's name a time or two, but mostly, people were making small talk. They discussed the heat that weekend. Yet another sign of climate change, they said. They talked about deer in their gardens and community theater and vacations they wanted to go on. The latest spreading strain of the virus, new boosters required of the vaccine. Sam and Elena had spent the last two years worried about bringing home illness, but their caution at this point didn't matter, did it? Sam's mask was pushed into her pants pocket. She could stand carelessly in this crowd. In one corner, her mother's co-workers bent together to show each other pictures on their phones of their grandchildren. Sam's mother would never be able to do that. Sam put more salad on her plate. Across the room, by the bar, she could see the top of Elena's head, the smooth blond fall of her hair.

"It's killing pets," someone near Sam said. "Etta Delaney told me their rabbit hutch was broken into. She's worried sick."

Someone else chimed in. "I told my husband he needs to stop going for long walks with the dog."

And then a third voice, authoritative. "While bears can target small animals, it's extremely unlikely that one would approach an adult man with a dog."

Sam turned. Past two strangers' shoulders, there she was: Madeline Pettit. It didn't seem possible. Madeline was holding a plastic cup of red wine. She was in her uniform, embroidered patch and all. She told the women she was talking to, "Only twenty Washington bear encounters have resulted in human injury in the last fifty years," and then caught Sam's eyes, and pressed her lips together, and excused herself to her conversation partners. She slipped past people to come up to Sam. Level as ever, Madeline said, "I was so sorry to hear of your mother's passing."

Everyone gave this same apology to Sam. She hadn't figured out yet what they expected her to say back. To this woman, especially—there was no reasonable response. Sam only said, "Why are you here?"

The compressed, solemn shape of Madeline's mouth. "I

was at Copper Kettle Farm this afternoon. They've been losing livestock. They mentioned your family, I told them we'd met, and they invited me to come offer condolences."

The owners of Copper Kettle Farm . . . Sam couldn't put that together. How had they known her mother? What had they said? And how could Madeline have accepted such an invitation, given by strangers, to this memorial for someone whom— "You didn't even know my mom."

"I know how destabilizing this can be. My own mother passed when I was in my twenties," Madeline said. "I came to extend support to you, but if you feel it's inappropriate for me to be here, I'll leave."

It hit Sam, then, the hot rush of humiliation: she was going to cry. Her eyes flooded. Her sinuses burned. She hadn't cried since they found their mother; Elena had done the breaking down for the both of them; Sam had held herself in check these many days, and now, horribly, Madeline Pettit, of all people, was making her fall apart. She tried to talk, but saliva was thick in her throat, she couldn't start. She had to try again. "Why." Sam stopped. She wasn't going to be able to get out the words. She turned away because she couldn't stand for Madeline to see her like this. There were napkins stacked on a table; Sam grabbed at some.

What was awful got worse. She felt the small, warm shape of Madeline's hand on her arm. "This is a difficult time," Madeline said, low. "You're overwhelmed. That

makes people act without thinking. It's completely under-
standable."

Sam had the wetting napkins pressed to her cheeks. Her
nose was clogged with snot. She cleared her throat, turned
back, and looked at Madeline. She didn't have it together
enough yet to say, *What are you talking about?*, but she looked
and hoped that Madeline received her meaning.

And Madeline did. She explained herself, steady and
consoling. "Leaving food out," she said, "baiting the bear,
hoping he might approach you—those behaviors have to
stop now. It's time to focus on your family."

Madeline thought Sam wanted the bear near her? Sam
would give anything not to be crying in front of this person. How could she have ever imagined the two of them
were tied? Madeline didn't belong here, not at this event,
not on this island, not anywhere where Sam would ever
be—she should never have come—and if Sam could hold
fast to that certainty, then maybe the tears would stop, but
she kept losing her grasp. The crying kept on. Because her
knowledge of Madeline's wrongness was mixed up with
some sense of betrayal. By Madeline or by Sam's own self.

Madeline was so close to seeing the truth. When Sam
was frightened, Madeline brought advice, bear spray. That
canister ruined everything, yes, chased Elena out of the
house on the night their mother died, but that wasn't Madeline's fault—or it was—or it wasn't—Sam didn't know,
her eyes were swelling, she was undone. Sam had to get

away, she knew, yet she had to admit too that when Madeline said she was here to give support, Sam's impulse was to fall at her feet and wrap her arms around the biologist's ankles. Madeline, she wanted to beg, protect us. My sister and I got lost in the woods. Please help us find our way home.

Throat clotted, Sam said, "You should go."

Madeline nodded. Then she said, "Sam, if there's anything about this that you need to sort out, write. Call." She squeezed Sam's arm, an even pressure. "I'm here to listen."

Sam pulled her body back. After days of sleeping separated from Elena by cold inches and years-old lies, she found Madeline's touch a comfort, and she hated herself for it, she hated the thin white nerves under her skin.

Madeline began to weave through the chatting crowd toward the club's door. Sam pushed her hands against her cheeks to try to make these tears go back in. Then she followed. The only other times Elena crossed paths with Madeline, she'd blown up at Sam after; if Madeline said something to set off Elena now, it would be a disaster. Madeline's ponytail bobbed toward the exit. Sam had to get between her and Elena. She shoved forward.

Bits of too-casual conversations kept catching at her. The state of the seaplanes used between here and Seattle, a duck laying eggs in someone's big backyard. For the millionth time in her life, Sam wished, with all her aching heart, that everyone else, their small talk and demands, would disappear. No more teachers or neighbors or former classmates, no other ways of being in the world. Nothing. Only Elena and Sam, safe in their old silence.

Madeline was only a few steps from Elena, who was facing away, toward the club's entrance. Don't notice her, Sam prayed, don't notice. Madeline, blessedly, passed. Only once the biologist reached the door did Sam see what Elena had been fixed on. Who had come in. Their mother's old boyfriend had arrived.

SAN JUAN WASN'T LARGE. FEWER THAN NINE THOUSAND people. Still, all this time, Sam and Elena had managed to avoid him. Sam thought, once, she'd seen him at the harbor, but she'd tracked that person for long minutes and concluded at last that it was some other brown-haired man who simply held his arms, overly muscled, the same way. She'd told Elena about the mix-up that night. "We don't need to worry about him anymore," Elena told her back then. "He's out of our lives." Elena spoke with the confidence that might come from his moving to San Francisco or falling down a well, and Sam took her words as a promise. She worked on forgetting him. She didn't keep watch for his posture anymore.

In the golf club, though, her mother's ex was so obviously, nauseatingly, himself that Sam couldn't see how she ever might have confused him for a different person. His neck, his shoulders, the slope of his jaw—years had passed, and his widow's peak had deepened, but Sam knew him in an instant. She knew him as well as she had on the last day he lived in their house. Her body knew his. The memory could never be let go.

She caught up with Elena, whose arms were folded across her chest. Sam wanted, like a child, to hold her big sister's hand. It wasn't in reach. She stood there.

This man had terrorized them. Told their mother he loved her and then screamed at her. Made their grandmother's house into a thorn-choked place. Forced Elena to get desperate enough to, for the last time, ask an outsider for help. He had altered them permanently; after him, their mother got sick, and Elena stopped trusting people, and Sam fixated on their escape.

He glanced over at the sisters and nodded. As if he was one more unremarkable visitor to the event, and hadn't, once upon a time, filled them with fear. He was shorter than Sam remembered—now that she'd seen a bear up on its hind legs, everything in comparison looked small—but he still scared the shit out of her. He did. More than any other monster on this island ever could.

Around them, people shuffled, talking of kids and schools and summer plans. They did what they had always done, which was ignore Sam and Elena's emergency, pretend the crisis away. Over the heads of neighbors, Sam spotted Danny Larsen holding a beer. He saw her, too, glanced at Elena, and frowned.

Their mother's ex had already moved ten feet into the club. Danny was making his way over.

Beside Sam, Elena trembled. The air between them shivered.

Danny got to their mother's ex and gripped his shoulder. Bent his head to say something that Sam couldn't read. Their mother's ex was facing away from them, but they could clearly see Danny, his teeth flashing within his beard as he spoke. Then he smiled, a small, sympathetic smile. He was taller than the older man and almost as broad. Whatever he was saying gave some push. The man turned toward the door. Together, he and Danny walked out.

"Oh my god," Sam said.

Elena took a step forward. Her arms were goosebumped. She didn't speak yet; Sam understood that she could not.

"Are they—?"

Elena shook herself. Her back moved like an animal's after a rain. Quiet enough that only Sam should hear, she said, "That's it. He left."

The relief. It was everything. The feeling of the bear spray in Sam's back pocket, the trigger releasing under her finger so the line of pepper arced out—each morning Sam had opened her eyes worrying that she wouldn't hear their mother's voice, and then she'd heard it, life continuing in the next room, that old vital sound—the day in high school they'd gotten home to find their mother's ex's things missing, their mother sitting alone in the living room, the light through the windows—every consolation Sam had ever had paled in comparison to this moment, the full-bodied joy of seeing this man gone so simply now. Even if it was temporary, even if it wasn't true. It filled her. She and Elena had survived crossing him again. He hadn't even gotten close to them. They were unscathed.

"God," Sam said. "He's even scarier than the bear."

Her sister whipped toward her. They should've been together in this moment, washed over by the same cool wave, but Elena only looked tight and furious. Her voice stayed low: "I don't know why I ever bothered," she said. "You don't understand a thing."

ELENA WENT STRAIGHTAWAY TO THE BATHROOM. "I'LL come with you," Sam said, reaching for her sister's wrist, but Elena shook her off. Sam said, "El, you—" and Elena said, "For a single minute since you were born, can you leave me alone?"

So Sam let her go. Elena slipped out of the room. She was going to hide in the club's single-occupancy bathroom, a space she'd probably wiped down thousands of times over the years, and defend to herself whoever or whatever she'd lashed out at Sam about: the man who'd hurt them, the animal that stalked them, the debts she'd accumulated and chosen to keep secret? No, Elena was right, Sam didn't understand. She couldn't. They'd spent their whole adult lives seemingly united in pursuit of a better future but somehow wound up here, orphaned, separate, stuck.

Sam forced her way to the club's exit. The dirt parking lot opened in front of her. She followed the building's edge, turned a corner, and sat heavy on the ground. Elena was a wall's thickness away. A universe apart. To Sam's right, acres of rolling green hills lay empty and perfectly mowed.

She sat there a long time. The day's heat was unbroken, and the sun sat heavy on her, a punishment. Under her, gravel pressed hard, points of pain on her butt and thighs; then, after a while, they vanished, and she felt nothing, only the numbness that precedes the shock of pins and needles, the rush of blood that was waiting for her when she stood up.

At last, footsteps. Sam turned to see Elena and found Danny Larsen's strong body instead.

"Hey," he said, folding himself down to sit next to her. "How are you holding up?"

"Pretty shitty," Sam said. "Yeah. If you're asking."

"I am."

He was the gentlest person she'd heard talk all day. If there were any tears left in her, they'd leak out now, but there weren't. She was emptied.

"Your mom was great," he said. "She used to bring us over zucchini from your garden."

Sam shook her head. Her mother bringing food to the Larsens—she couldn't picture the time. "When was that?"

"In elementary school, maybe? When we were kids. My mom would make bread from it. Muffins."

"I don't remember our mom in that garden. I always thought it was our grandmother's thing."

He shrugged. "She definitely knew how to get vegetables out of it. Tomatoes, she'd bring, too."

His bent leg was close to hers. An inch away. Less. Last month, she would have recoiled at the thought of being knee to knee with Danny, but in this moment, there were few things she wanted more. She was sweating in this weather, but he smelled good. Soapy. Clean laundry. Childhood memories.

"She was so young," he said. "It isn't fair."

Sam had to agree with that. "No," she said. "It isn't."

He didn't say anything for a while after, and she was grateful. In quiet, they watched the cut grass shiver across the green.

Eventually, he spoke again. "Do you know where your sister is?"

"She's in the bathroom," Sam said. Bitter: "She wanted time alone."

Elena would call that tone of voice immature. Danny didn't comment on it, though. He rested his head against the wall of the clubhouse and let it go. The kid he'd been in school was blustering, foolish, too loud, too much, but Danny now was none of those things. He was just right.

Inside the club, Elena was probably washing her face clean of tears. Preparing to offer more niceties to the people who didn't know them but whom, for some reason, she felt obliged to entertain. She was, in her grief, acting like someone Sam didn't recognize, but then again Sam didn't recognize herself, either. The girl sitting with Danny Larsen. Soothed by him. Too strange.

She opened her mouth to bring up what she thought she'd never discuss with anyone outside her home. "How'd you know?"

"Know what?"

"When he came in," she said. Her mother's ex. "That you needed to make him leave."

He paused. Giving that question the deliberation it deserved. Then: "I saw your faces."

The rest of the people in there had milled around them, looked right over them, thought only of themselves. How had Danny, out of everyone, seen?

"I remember that time," he said. "When he lived with you. When he moved out."

In the lot beside them, a car backed out of a parking space. Scattered stones crunched under its tires. Sam couldn't look at Danny. He was too near. She leaned her head back, too, and gazed at the hot sky. That time—she and Elena came home from school every day not knowing what they would find when they unlocked their front door. Their mother wooed or hunted. That man cycling through threats. To think, now, that Danny had seen through the walls of their house—to think he'd known.

These past couple months, Ben had told Sam, as he pressed himself close, how much he cared, but it rang false in every instance. For all the time he'd spent inside her, they had no intimacy; she'd tried not to let him find out the most important things about her, and hardly paid attention to whatever he shared about himself. It was embarrassing, frankly, that he kept pursuing the idea that they liked each other, when they had no idea what there was to like. Real care was something else entirely. A more rare beast. It was growing up alongside each other, watching one another. It was the ability to hear what wasn't said.

Not looking at Danny, Sam reached out toward him. His leg was so close. She touched her fingers to his thigh.

He moved his leg away.

She pulled her hand back. "Sorry."

"No," he said, "you're good, don't worry."

"Sorry," she said again. Shook her head. Stupid. Her hands were in her lap.

"No, I—" He stopped. She could picture it: his sincere, sad face, eyebrows pushed together in pity for her. He'd come out here because he felt bad for her. His poor pathetic neighbor. She'd gotten it all wrong.

"Forget about it," she said. God knew she would try.

"Sam . . ." His distress was audible. She wished she could bury herself under the dirt of this parking lot. This was pure humiliation. "It's not . . . I'm with Elena."

She turned to him. "What?"

His face was as tortured as she'd expected, but it didn't make sense to her, not his expression in this moment, not his words. "Elena and I are together."

Sam opened her mouth and shut it.

He said, "For months now. We dated in school, and then we got back together last year, after things got crazy, the lockdown. I know it's been tough on your family . . . She hasn't wanted to tell anyone, she thought it'd be too much. But I'm sorry. I'm sorry you didn't know."

"That's impossible," Sam said.

He winced. His big, handsome face was only a foot from hers, and she couldn't take it in, it was a stranger's. Was he insane? Harboring some delusion? Had he gotten obsessed with Elena when they were seniors, after she turned him down, and ended up pretending they were having an affair?

Sam needed to make it clear to him. "No, you're not."

"That's how I knew about . . . She told me back then. We'd just started talking. Sophomore year."

Not true. Against her will, though, Sam remembered tenth-grade Elena confiding in her science teacher, Elena entertaining the idea that a social worker might set things right. Elena had behaved then in ways she never had since. Maybe Elena had . . . said something to him, let some secret slip . . . but it couldn't have gone any further than that. Sam was sure. She had to be, otherwise she might sit here, in this dirty lot, and lose her mind.

He kept talking. She wanted to tell him to shut up. "I always had a huge crush on her, but she had a rule about not getting into any serious relationship. She said she'd seen what it did to your mom and she never wanted that. So we just talked. For ages. We texted a lot. Sometimes we did homework together during free periods. When she started working here, I'd hang in the grill during her shifts. And after we graduated, we . . ." He trailed off. They . . . ? Sam stared at him. They what?

"You what?"

He grimaced. "You should really talk with her about this."

"I'll talk to my sister about whatever I want," Sam said. Her sister, who was hiding in a bathroom to get away from her. Her sister who'd remortgaged their property.

"All I mean is that we're with each other," he said. "And she's the one for me. I can't imagine ever being with anyone else."

The walks Elena went off on alone. The dog that barked in the background of her phone calls. The information Danny always seemed to have about Sam's family. His coming over to fix their siding, at Elena's request.

They were together. All this time.

Danny said, "She prefers to keep it quiet. She's private."

"I know that," Sam said.

"Okay."

"Because she and I don't waste our time with other people. We're trying to get out of here."

Danny did look at her with pity then. "Okay," he repeated. His voice made it horrendous and clear. He knew Elena exactly as she was now—the new Elena Sam had argued with this week, the one who'd decided they couldn't afford to leave. So no apology text from Elena was going to pop up on Sam's phone; Elena wasn't going to take back what she'd said in their kitchen; Elena didn't see the sisters ever getting their final ferry ride. He knew.

SHE FOUND ELENA IN A CORNER OF THE CROWDED CLUB with Kristine. "I'm going home," Sam told her sister. Kristine, white wine in hand, frowned.

"You can't," Elena said. "We have another hour here."

"I don't care. I'm leaving."

Kristine, who usually only existed in Sam's life as a vibration on Elena's cellphone, spoke up. Sam couldn't remember the last time she'd heard Kristine's voice. It was thin and high and pointless. "Wouldn't your mom want you guys to be doing this stuff together?"

Sam slitted her eyes at Kristine. "I'm sorry, who are you?"

"Lower your voice," Elena hissed. "And don't you talk to her that way."

Beside Elena, Kristine murmured, "It's okay, it's okay."

Sam couldn't look at her. Did Kristine already know about Danny? Had she helped cover for Elena's sneaking around all this time? "She's the one who shouldn't be talking," Sam said. "Has she ever even met Mom?" But then— what did Sam know, maybe Kristine had, maybe Kristine and their mother were best friends who played gin rummy and watched game shows together while Sam was at work. Everyone else seemed to have a secret life. Why not this girl, too?

Sam could not stand it. The people around them snacking. The bright lights overhead and the wall of windows showcasing the manicured green outside. The absolute fakeness of it all. For years, in the midst of the mindless buzz produced by every other person on this island, Sam had believed she had one good, real thing: her sister. But Elena had been faking it, too.

"I'm done," Sam said. "See you later."

She pushed her way out of the club door and Elena followed. The side of the clubhouse where Sam had sat with Danny was empty now. Sam hurried through the parking lot. Behind her, Elena called after.

"Sam. Sam. Sammy." Elena grabbed Sam's elbow. "Stop."

Sam whirled around. "You stop."

"I'm the one of us who's acting halfway normal," Elena said. "Meanwhile you're stomping around and screaming at my friends. You can't pretend to be a regular person for three hours? Is that really too much to ask?"

"Oh," Sam said. "Oh. I see. You want me to be normal and regular and pretend, just like you."

Elena had let go of Sam's arm but her words still clenched tight. "I want you to keep it together for the length of our mother's memorial. At least try."

"Let me follow your lead," Sam said. "Elena, the role model. Why don't you show me what to do. Insist to everyone that nothing's wrong? Put us so far in debt that you say we'll never get out of it? Lie a million times in a row to your own sister? Sleep with Danny fucking Larsen?"

Even as Sam said it, she prayed for a denial. Elena looking struck and shocked: *what are you talking about, I would never . . .* Instead Elena's expression firmed. She looked exactly as indignant as she had the moment before, only more. It was true, then. She was with him. She had been hiding it from Sam.

Sam said, "How could you."

In the yellow sun, Elena was whitewashed stone. Almost as pale as their mother had been, when they found her. "How could I what? Attempt, for one second, to feel good, instead of sacrificing my entire existence to you and Mom?"

"I never asked for you to—"

"You did worse than ask," Elena said. "You expected. Both of you. Forever. That I would be this perfect person, never weak, never with a complaint, like I was made only to take care of this family and didn't have a single need of my own—"

"No, sorry, that's bullshit," Sam said. "You were the one who insisted on doing it this way, you're the one who said no relationships."

Elena actually scoffed then. The sound of it, ugly, didn't fit her. "When I was in high school. When he was living with us. That was— Sam, that was the sort of thing a kid says when they're scared, not a rule for living the rest of your life."

"No." Back then, they'd set all sorts of rules. They'd come to an understanding, together, that Sam had spent every day since depending on.

"We're not children anymore, making up stories about what our grown-up selves might be. We're adults. I have friends, I have responsibilities, I sleep with people."

"With Danny Larsen." Sam was the one sneering now. It seemed more natural, coming from her.

Elena rolled her eyes. "And I don't tell you about any of it for this reason: because you can't handle it."

"That's not true."

"I know you've never liked Danny. You're rude to him. Whenever he spoke to us, even when we were kids, you'd insult him or talk in this mock polite voice. You can be so condescending. I don't need you to act that way to me about how I spend my time and who I spend it with."

"That's ridiculous," Sam said. "I'm fine with Danny." Her fingers on his leg. His eyes soft, his beard curling. "And you know about Ben and me and— I mean, I tell you everything."

Elena shrugged. "Okay. Well. I don't."

Her shoulders had risen so easily. Behind her, a few people trickled out of the club, heading to their cars, leaving dry dirt to puff from the ground under their feet. A row of golf carts sat empty. In the light from the evening sun, Elena's beauty, her exhaustion, was clearer than ever. Faint lines drew from her nostrils toward her mouth.

"You think I'm not supportive of you," Sam said. "That I make all these demands. But you're wrong. I'm actually . . . I don't care what supposed friends you have. You're never going to find anyone, ever, who's more dedicated to you than I am. I've been putting in all my effort for years to make your dream come true."

And this was love. Wasn't it? They might argue with each other or waste their time with random men, but this bond was what really mattered. Their mother was gone, and this narrowing family, this long and precious sisterhood, was all Sam and Elena had left.

Elena didn't recognize that, though. She only said, "What dream?"

Sam said, "To leave."

Elena shook her head. She actually shook her head. "That's not going to happen."

"I get it," Sam said, "you explained it to me, the house, the debt, we— I get it. But you can't give up. I'm not giving up. We can make it out, somehow, together."

"You're not listening," Elena said. "I'm not saying I don't think we can do it. I'm telling you I don't want to."

Her sister. Her guide. Elena here, on San Juan Island, forever. Serving up Caesar salads alongside Kristine, paying the minimum on her accounts, sneaking over to the Larsens' to make out with Danny, never doing anything beyond this. She'd told Sam before how tired she was, and she'd been right—Sam hadn't understood. Sam, sustained through years by faith in what was coming, had no idea, even as Elena described it, how dire the situation had gotten.

All the times, even just today, Sam's heart had broken. Of all of those, this one devastated her the most. Her sister faltering. "Don't say that."

"Why not? It's true." In this parking lot, the woman Elena might age to be was made obvious. Thin, pale, and, eventually, formerly beautiful. Her hair would turn white as their mother's never had. Day by day, this island would take her down. Elena said, "God knows this isn't perfect, but there's something here that's nowhere else. Something I love."

You're in love with Danny Larsen? Sam had the urge to shriek. Then she realized: no. Elena wasn't talking in this bizarre way because she was moved by the boy next door. Something else had pushed her to this point. A thing stranger, wilder. Bestial.

THE WALK HOME FROM THE CLUB FORCED SAM TO GO IN Elena's footsteps, along Elena's daily commute, on American Camp Trail. Sam moved stricken. She traced the border of the golf course, the edges of luxury properties, and the turn onto Cattle Point. The trail dipped into the woods. Lines of ants crossed the soil in front of her. Spiderwebs strung across her face and arms. She had to rub her skin free. She itched.

Roots rolled under her sneakers. Elena's words were in her mind. The grief of the last week had pushed both sisters too far. What Sam might've thought had been the worst times of their lives (surviving under their mother's boyfriend, learning their mother's illness was terminal) were recast as mild trials, compared to this. At least for those, they'd had each other. Now they were apart.

But then again they'd made it through other periods of separation. They had. Though Sam didn't like to think of those. When Elena graduated to middle school and left Sam by herself in fifth grade, or to high school and left Sam in eighth. When she finished high school and moved on to the golf club, while Sam counted down the days left as a senior. Over and over, Elena had stepped away from their pairing— Elena was asked to dances, tried out for the National Ocean Sciences Bowl, told Sam the club wasn't hiring anymore— but she had always come back to Sam. Eventually.

Toward the end of elementary school, one girl, Chloe McRary, had shown off her nails in the cafeteria: neon yellow with fine green tips. Sam had been so excited. "Did you get those done at Treasures?" Sam asked. "My mom works there." And Chloe, her nasty little friends sitting alongside, had squealed. "Your mom works there?" Chloe said. "That's so embarrassing."

Sam hadn't known until then that she ought to be embarrassed. Her body felt like it had been lit on fire. She spent that whole school year alone, watching the other girls gather in circles and whisper, laugh over the sleepovers they'd shared, talk about what she wasn't acquainted with. Their parents, their vacations, their housekeepers, their pets. Their fluorescent manicures, hardened with mysterious shames.

Elena told Sam today that she didn't listen, didn't understand. If that was true, it wasn't for lack of Sam's early effort. She had spent lunch periods, long days, and entire seasons of her young life at the edges of other kids' crowds, attempting to grasp but never catching what those kids actually meant. That's so embarrassing, Chloe had said. Was it? Why? Sam asked Elena about it later. Elena only said, with the authority of a twelve-year-old speaking about eleven-year-olds, "Who cares what they're saying? They don't matter anyway."

So Sam adopted that same philosophy. She and Elena were essential; everyone outside of their family was simply a bother. She stopped loitering near her classmates at lunch, at recess, or in the locker room. She didn't join any sports teams or the choir. When she finally got to middle school, she made sure to line up her schedule as much as possible with Elena's, so they could walk the halls together between periods. If not, Sam walked alone. By the time she got to Friday Harbor High, Sam's reputation was set: she was a loser. Poor and weird and sullen. Refused to participate in routine conversation, rude to anyone who approached. Sam broadcast the message conveyed to her by her older sister: no one else mattered, so who cared?

Elena behaved differently, though. In high school, Sam saw it: Elena wasn't an outcast or a freak. The kids in different cliques were friendly; the teachers in Sam and Elena's shared electives called on her; their guidance counselor even told her he'd write her a recommendation letter for college. Elena, meanwhile, smiled, nodded, shrugged, and drifted away. She stayed graceful in her disregard. Though she accepted nothing, she humored anything. Everyone liked her for that quality. Watching, Sam feared that Elena might quietly detach from her, too.

But Elena hadn't. Despite these moments of seeming distance, Elena was there, at home, washing their dishes and joking with Sam at the end of the day. And in this moment, too, Sam had to believe that Elena would return to their sisterhood. Friends and lovers and assorted duties would pass out of Elena's existence, but Sam wouldn't. She never could.

Branches striped the ground with shadows. The trail bumped down. On Sam's right, a car whooshed by. On her left, then, another kind of movement. Something stepping in the woods.

She turned. The brush was thick. Trees, bushes, pine needles, wide leaves, a fence marking a property line, filmy webs and orange flower buds. No unusual motion. Had she imagined it? But: no. Again.

A brown mass between far trunks.

"I don't have anything for you," Sam said. The bear, in the distance, didn't budge. She raised her voice: "Get out of here. Leave."

Between the trees, a shift. Not a departure.

"Go," Sam shouted. "Go on. Get." Did it smell Elena on her? Was it lingering in the hope of tracking her sister? "She's not coming."

The thing stayed.

Sam stepped toward it. It had to be two hundred feet away—what was she trying to do, intimidate it by inches? Grasses crushed under her feet. Tall, tender, alive. She bent over, picked up a loose branch, and threw it in the bear's direction, but the branch vanished into undergrowth.

"Go. Would you go? Get away."

It stayed. It waited there, in front of her, patient as a groom at the altar. And the fury overwhelmed.

Sam went up to the plank fence that separated her from the stretch of green the bear occupied. She climbed onto its bottom rung. Sweat rolled down her spine. She shook. Until now, she'd spent her every encounter with this animal consumed by fear, but her fear had left at last, she was filled with nothing but anger. In a more fair universe, this thing would've never come here, but in this world everything was terrible and their mother, at only fifty-one, had died alone of a heart attack, and Elena and Sam were stuck, and Elena liked it, and this bear stared after them every single day as if it relished their position. It looked at them as entertainment or as prey. With the edge of the plank pressing hard against her soles, Sam screamed at it. "Leave us alone." Her throat hurt to make the sound. "Get out of here. I'm not going to let you take her."

Way back in the woods, the thing receded.

Sam wobbled on the fence. She had to lean over and grip the top plank, thigh-level, for balance. She kept shaking. All these years, she'd tried to follow what her sister told her was right. She had even walked into the forest to greet a bear because Elena encouraged it. But Elena was wrong now. It was obvious. She'd been wrong, today, in the way she insulted Sam; she'd been wrong to organize this memorial; she had done wrong for years by keeping secrets that drove a wedge between them; she was wrong to make a vi-

sion for a new life and then let it go. Elena had gotten off
track, somehow. She messed up. She loved a grizzly bear.
Sam, though, had not lost her focus. From this vantage
point, Sam could see the grassy island, the place the animal
had stood, and her sister's failings. She saw, at last, how to
proceed.

After Elena, newly graduated, went full-time at the club,
Sam was terrified that her sister was moving on from the
life of their family. Elena came home then talking about her
co-workers. She seemed to engage with them in a way she
never fully had with the kids they grew up alongside. She
moved out of their shared bedroom into the living room
and spent more time on her phone. Sam's prospects were
curtailed by a high school schedule, but Elena's were enlarg-
ing, and Sam worried that soon they would be big enough
to make a sister small. So one day, after the last bell rang,
Sam walked from the school campus to the golf course, entered the dusty parking lot, and sat on the hood of their car.
She did her homework there while she waited for Elena to
clock out. It took hours. Finally Elena emerged from the
door of the grill. She was in a clot with two other servers.
When she saw Sam, she straightened, grinned.

They got in the car together that day. Elena was in the
driver's seat. She smelled of grease, alcohol, and sugar. Her
eyes were bright. "I was bored so I thought I'd come visit,"
Sam said.

"Aren't you a sweetie," Elena said. She waved out the
window to one of the other servers, then buckled herself in.

"It's fun here?"

"Yeah. The people are fun, yeah."

"Should I work here, too? After school?"

Elena rolled out of the parking space. Her voice was casual. "If you want."

Sam watched her sister navigating the dirt road from the club like she'd been born to it. "I'm just trying to sort out, you know, what'll happen after my senior year ends. What'll we do?"

"You've got time. Don't stress."

"I'm serious, though," Sam said. Elena glanced from the road to her for a second before flicking her eyes back. Sam felt, in her throat, the slightest tremor. She had spent that whole day sitting alone in classes, surrounded by people who had nothing in common with her, stuck in a routine she by that point despised. If she couldn't go backwards, to when their mother was perfectly healthy and the sisters spent their days walking wild over the island's mysteries, then she wanted to go forward to something as good. Something better. "I don't want us to split up," she said. Her voice cracked at the last words. She could tell Elena heard. "What are we going to do?"

That very night, when Sam came out to sit with her on the sofa before sleep, Elena laid out their new vision: working for a while, taking care of their mother, then selling the house, setting themselves up somewhere private and calm. Sam knew that Elena had invented this answer to comfort her. That didn't mean it wasn't true.

Elena had come back to Sam, to the bond they shared, because Sam demanded it of her. She would do it again now. Sorrow, money, and this goddamn creature had pulled Elena away, but Sam wasn't going to let her go any further. Elena confessed she loved other things, but in the end, she had to love her sister more.

So Sam would set them right one last time. Put Elena's distractions behind them—death, debt, Danny Larsen. The bear. Elena had called it the best thing that ever happened to her, but once it was gone, Elena would see what other bests were waiting. She would return to Sam.

THE NEXT DAY, SAM'S MANAGER ASKED HER TO WORK another double. Sam agreed right away. She needed what fourteen hours of work would give her: both the pay and the time. Before the sun came up, the passenger deck was quiet. She could focus. Sitting in a plastic chair bolted to the floor in the empty galley, she tapped on her phone. The boat's engines rumbled up through her shoes.

Ben slid into the seat across from her. "Hey."

Sam glanced up from her screen, where she'd been skimming over the message she'd typed to Madeline. *Hi, I just want to let you know that the bear has been taking food from my sister and following her to and from work. And as you heard it's also been killing people's animals. So it's a big problem. Its behavior has been escalating and is dangerous and you all do need to deal with it ASAP.*

Ben's eyes were dark underneath. "You worked last night?" she asked. He nodded. "When was the last time you slept?"

He blinked at her, heavy-lidded, and smiled. "I took a nap around one. Look at you, so thoughtful."

She returned to her phone to tap the send button. The email vanished. The wind across the channel would carry it to Madeline now. "That's me."

The ferry hummed. The noise it made pushing forward filled the quiet between them, making it familiar, bearable. She didn't mind Ben being there as long as he didn't open his mouth. Under the smell of the galley—coffee grounds, microwaves—Sam could smell him. Ben's deodorant and laundry detergent and cologne. Old, delicious cigarette smoke. The base pleasure of a proximate body.

Of course he ruined it. "How are you doing?" he asked. "How was the service?"

"Great. A laugh riot."

Ben let his breath out through his teeth. What did he want her to say? That Sam had sobbed, and seen her mother's ex, and touched Danny's leg like a creep, and gotten into the worst fight of her life with Elena? That she'd ended the day screaming at a grizzly bear, swearing to destroy it before it destroyed them?

She and Ben used to sit up here, when her customers were few and his tasks had been momentarily handled, and play at sharing secrets. He'd talk about roaming his neighborhood, smashing things and emptying spray-paint cans with his friends. And she'd give him her fondest San Juan memories: the beaches, the farms, the forests, the wanderings. What it had been to grow up thinking the whole world was an island, and she and Elena its rulers, its saltwater-crusted queens.

She had nothing left to say to him, though. She couldn't look backwards anymore. Sam needed, alone, to concentrate on the future. How to salvage it now.

"I think I'm going to leave the ferry after this season," Ben said.

Sam lifted her face from the screen. "Yeah?"

He shrugged. The bags under his eyes made him look less boyish, more adult. A cord plucked in Sam's gut. He had been fun—and he was handsome—Ben, in his gloves and cap and vest, hauling rope out on the deck, lifting her onto him.

He said, "I don't know. Feels like time to move on."

"I get that feeling," Sam said.

"I was thinking about heading back toward Oregon. A guy I know is working on a hemp grow there and he says the pay is ridiculous."

All he'd see that she wouldn't. She said, "Cool."

Ben's body was curved to fit the scoop of the chair. His legs were spread, boots flat on the floor. The windowpanes that surrounded them trembled in their frames. "Want to come?"

Quiet as it was on the boat at this time of day, Sam must've misheard him. "What?"

"Do you want to come with me? In the fall?"

She didn't— "I—"

"You're always talking about leaving," Ben said. "I know, with everything with your mom, you've had to stay. But now . . . maybe things have changed."

She didn't know what to say.

He talked on. "I like you. We have a good time together. Don't we? And down there, there are jobs, I've got a place for us. Maybe this is what you've been waiting for."

Sam said, "I can't. No."

His expression changed. The boyishness came back. She hadn't known Ben as a kid, but this might have been what he'd looked like—vulnerable this way. "Okay."

"It's very . . ." She was floundering, trying to find her words. She had never expected this from him. What she wouldn't give, right now, for a long, irritating interruption from a European tourist family, inquiring about lavender and natural wines. "It's nice of you to offer, but, Ben, I'm not . . . We've only known each other a couple months."

Ben sat up. His back broke away from the line of the chair. "I know that. Okay? I'm not asking you to marry me. I'm just . . . There's more to the world than this, Sam. You don't like it here? You don't have to sit in the same spot hating it. You can do things. Meet people. Change your mind once in a while. Try stuff. And as pointless as you think it is for me to like you, I do, and if you wanted to try stuff together, I would."

Sam had another twinge, then. In her stomach. Her chest. Within her, something tiny, eager, vibrated: why not? The two of them could dock in Anacortes and walk off this boat. The sun would be rising by then. The whole Pacific coast, green trees shot through with sun, would open itself to her. Ben made it sound easy. She could do it, exactly as he said. She could change.

It was only a twinge, though. She moved her eyes off his
body and the feeling disappeared. Ben got up. She faced
away. A customer was coming toward the cash register, and
Sam stood, too, to tend to that. By the time she finished
ringing them out, an apple and a pastry, Ben was gone.

The sky was lightening. Under the counter, Sam refreshed her email. And though she'd expected it might take
hours before Madeline even read her message, the phone
buzzed in her palms, and there, to her shock, was a response.
She held her breath and opened it. *Hi Sam,* Madeline had
written. What was she doing up? *Thank you for your candor. I
can't tell you how much I appreciate it.* Sam couldn't read the
sentences fast enough.

> I completely understand your concern. On our end,
> we will pursue trapping, tagging, and relocation.
>
>   To be frank, though, the problem is your sister.
> Removal will not correct anything if the bear's taught
> that humans are his best food source; relocated bears
> almost always return. He will come back, get labeled
> a threat, and be killed.
>
>   The only real remedy is for your sister to change
> her behavior. What she is doing is not only unwise
> but illegal. While I can refer this to the sheriff's
> office—the maximum penalty is ninety days in

jail—I doubt that would resolve the matter. In our experience, working with, not against, members of the public is most effective.

I would very much like to collaborate with you on this, Sam. You are, after all, the person closest to Elena.

Would you and your sister be interested in coming to our office in Mill Creek? We would host you while the three of us discuss how to proceed. We'd cover your travel costs. I imagine you both would benefit from some distance from home right now. And you and I can work together to help your sister see. This way might be ideal, I think. We can save a life.

Sam's mouth was open. Her tongue was dry, she realized. She swallowed, and she thought: absolutely fucking not. Sam had written to Madeline because Madeline's team was supposed to terrify the bear off this island. Show up with dogs and tags and tranquilizer darts, chase away this monster like the state had spooked the man out of Sam and Elena's house years before. Afterward, Sam and Elena would be left to clean up the mess, but that was fine, they'd done it before, they could sort themselves out again. That, Sam knew. But this? This was unimaginable.

Their future was meant to be Seattle, Sol Duc, wide-open California, skiing and dating and ease. Not *Mill Creek*. And certainly not with Madeline. Jail, she'd said. Was she

insane? What had Sam been thinking, writing to her? Sam
didn't even allow herself the twinge she'd felt with Ben's
proposal (because if Madeline could lift them out of here,
guide Sam through, talk sense into Elena, if she could actually help—?) No, no. Instead, in seconds, she had her reply:
My sister is not the problem. People like you are. Stay away.

Sent. The sun was barely up and Sam had already had
enough of everyone else's bullshit. To pacify herself, she
navigated to a survey open in her browser. She had a couple
bars of service, she could knock it out in the next few minutes. Reflexively, she tapped through questions about her
taste in snacks and weekly grocery budget. Soon she would
be done with this. Their future was coming. There was no
option left than for Sam, on San Juan, to get them free.

THE TOO-HOT SUN WAS DOWN BY THE TIME SAM GOT home from work. The squares of the house's open windows were mostly dark, with only a glow from the living room. Elena must've already finished cleaning for the night. When Sam shut the car door, its sound lifted to the trees. A bat flew overhead.

Madeline had emailed back later that morning. A message as curt as Sam's had been: *Intervention with Elena is your best and only way out*. The bear expert. Please. What did that woman know of them?

Sam unlocked the front door. Before her shoes were off, she heard Elena from the sofa: "Late night."

Sam slid her second sneaker off her heel. "Not that late. Just a long one."

"Come sit," her sister said.

The house was so still these days without the rush of oxygen flowing from their mother's bedroom. Its floor creaked under Sam's feet as she crossed to the living room. The walls sighed. Sam settled on the sofa, where Elena sat, pillow on her lap, looking thin and worn and regal, her hair in a post-shower bun.

"You must've gotten a lot done today," Elena said.

"Not really. Same old." Sam's legs hurt. No matter how many breaks she took to sit while on the boat, after a double, her body felt pressed down, spine grinding and feet pounded into bone. She shifted on the cushion. Her tailbone ached. If they asked her the next day to work these same hours, she'd decline, she thought, then thought again—maybe not, wouldn't it help them to have the money . . .

"I don't know about that," Elena said. "I certainly had an interesting day. Thanks to you."

The dread. Oh, God, it sent Sam right to childhood. Their mother, working, wasn't always around, and when she was she didn't have the energy for small disciplines, so Elena took over that responsibility on her behalf. The reprimands: be careful, Elena would say, watch out, what are you doing, didn't I warn you? When Sam made a mistake, sticking a pebble up one nostril or biting a first-grade classmate's arm on the playground, Elena would launch in. *Sammy, what did I say* . . . The tone of the older sister, which communicated love, certainly, and dedication, but also such deep disappointment, fatigue stemming from superiority. Even now, a grown woman, Sam squirmed under that sound.

There were a million possibilities for blame. Something

Sam did wrong at the memorial? The way she tried to touch Danny, or insulted Kristine? Her screams at the bear? Or had Elena somehow seen the messages on Sam's phone? Quick, Sam flipped through guilts, but there was nothing most obvious to start apologizing for. "What happened?" she asked.

Elena's mouth twisted up. Only the lamp on the side table was on, making her features exaggerated, her eyes sink deeper than ever into their sockets. "We had a visit from a sheriff's deputy this afternoon."

Sam's stomach dropped. "We what?"

"A man from the sheriff's office stopped by," Elena said. "He let me know it's against state law to feed wild carnivores, and he issued me a five-hundred-dollar fine."

Five hundred dollars. Sam's work today, gone, like that—fourteen hours on the clock only got her three hundred and thirty dollars, before taxes—so this would take everything Elena had made at the club today, too—this took everything. Forget getting ahead on the mortgage. They were further behind than ever.

Elena said, "I wonder why he thought I was feeding animals?"

The dread. The guilt. The horror of it all. "Yesterday, at the club, that woman Madeline was there, and she told me she thought we were baiting it, so I emailed her this morning, and I said—"

Elena shook her head. She used to stand in the place of Sam's mother, but now she was the sole leader of their household. In August, she would turn thirty; she waited up when Sam came home late; she issued punishments. It didn't seem to matter how desperate Sam became to disrupt what was going on—Elena was in charge.

Sam said, "El, I'm trying to help you, I'm trying to help us. I'm sorry. I'm just trying to get this thing out of here."

"He doesn't want to leave. Neither do I. You do. So you go, Sam."

Hearing this from her sister was more shocking than the notion of the sheriff. "What?"

"You go," Elena said. "Move out. It's overdue, anyway. You've wanted all this time to leave, so do it, already. Stop hanging around messing with my life. Go make your own."

IN HER BEDROOM, ALONE, SAM WORKED. THERE WAS NOTH-
ing else she was better at than this. She had perfected,
over years, the ability to set herself to an ugly task. One
month earlier, this bear had appeared at their door and ruined everything, but Sam was not going to let its influence
last one minute longer. Once the bear was gone, the sisters
would, in their long love and mutual grief, mend. Sam had
messed up, yes, and she might've lost Elena's trust, but she
wasn't going to lose Elena herself. She wasn't going to let an
animal take her sister away.

First she emailed Madeline Pettit to tell her to fuck off.
At least on that front, Elena had been right all along: no
outsider could ever help them. Allowing Madeline's in-
volvement had been a blunder. Sam had learned her lesson.

She texted Danny, then, though it was late, a Sunday
night, and awkward. Who cared? If he really was so dedicated to her sister, he could put up with a text message to
prove it. Sam's innards felt coated in cooled metal. The rage
she'd carried had turned from fire to something cold and
hard. Inside her, certainty. She wasn't going to give up

Elena, even if Elena declared she was willing to give up Sam.

His reply made the phone vibrate in Sam's hands. She tapped out a rapid response: he had once told her he would lend them his dog, so she would like the dog, please, and his gun. She was forced to wait longer than she would've liked for him to write back. While he, next door, took his time, she searched online for what scared bears away. Loud noises. Sudden movements. One website recommended a water balloon coated in peanut butter and filled with bleach. That sounded good, she thought, and then Danny responded, saying he'd heard from Elena that the bear stuff was getting complicated with the sheriff, and he didn't want to get in the middle of anything. Coward. Fool.

Sam pressed her phone to her forehead and deliberated. Then she put her thumbs back to the screen to hammer out her appeal. Had he seen this bear? He hadn't? Sam had. It approached Elena—it was aggressive. Had Elena told him that? The scientists from the state had warned Elena against calling it to her, because that would make it behave more riskily, but she'd persisted, and that's why the sheriff had gotten involved. Did he know that? He didn't. *Danny,* Sam wrote, *you say to trust her, and I do, I always have, but this is different. This is dangerous. If you care about Elena, you'll understand why we have to keep her away from it. It's got to be chased off before something terrible happens.*

The Danny they'd grown up with would ignore all this in favor of school dances and soccer practice. But the Danny

who'd fixed their siding—well. Sam waited to see. She expected a response from that sweet, trusting, bearded man,
the one she'd sat in quiet beside. Instead she got a text from
the person she'd suspected and never yet spoken to, the one
who hid between the two far-apart versions of himself
Danny showed the world. Here was the real one. Jealous.
The one capable of doing harm. *No I didn't know that,* he
wrote back. *But to be honest I guess some part of me's not surprised
to find out. I know she hides stuff/has been hiding stuff. She's been
more distant lately. I could tell. Yeah you're right Sam.* She read
that message cold and clear. It came as comfort, in a way, to
have this confirmation: people who could grasp what Sam
was saying would only come from this particular place. He
wrote, *El needs us even if she can't admit it yet. The way she acts
about this thing is crazy. It is time for someone to make it stop.*

THEY WENT OUT TOGETHER, SHE AND DANNY, WHILE Elena was at work the next day. Sam had worked the morning shift so she was back home by lunch. He met her on the road with his dog at his side and a handgun holstered on his waist. Sam frowned down. "I thought you'd have a big rifle or something."

"It's not hunting season," he said. "Washington may be an open carry state, but if I waved a rifle around the streets of Friday Harbor in June, I'm pretty sure a deputy would show up."

The dog sniffed the road at Danny's feet. In Danny's holster, the gun was compact, promising. "Can I hold it?" Sam asked.

He grimaced. "Have you ever held one before?" She shook her head. "Not right now," he said. "Maybe later."

They had time. They were prepared to wait as long as it took. Side by side, they walked to the end of their road, crossed Cattle Point, and climbed onto the trail. The dog panted happily underneath. Danny, petting it, asked Sam why she imagined a hunting rifle. They weren't hunting, were they? She could tell that, though he was with her, he was hesitating again, picking over his words as carefully as he had the night before when he was delaying his texts. Before he let his dread of losing Elena peek through. The dread was still there, though. The truest, hungriest part of him. She spoke to that. No, she told him, they weren't hunting. They were intimidating. They were there to frighten away what had attempted first to frighten them.

Under the trees on the trail, the air was shaded, cooler. The weekend's heat had finally broken. The dog pissed on a heap of roots that rose from the ground. They walked north, slowly, toward the golf club, and didn't speak to each other. Sam concentrated on watching for movement in the far brush.

"Do you really think we'll see it?" Danny asked.

His talking likely didn't help them. But: "Yes." The dog had run ahead on the path, but came back, goofy and grinning, at the sound of their voices. A car passed. Sam said, "We could've brought some food to attract it, I guess. Elena does that."

He sighed.

Sam had considered, as they texted through the logistics, asking him whether they could tie some bait to the dog's collar, to make sure the bear would be drawn their way. But she'd rethought that idea. The last thing she and Elena needed was to be sued by the Larsens for endangering their puppy. His mother seemed the type to overreact. It wasn't worth mentioning to him, then, the schemes that

Sam had come up with and disregarded before landing on this afternoon's plan. The best way they had of finding it was following Elena. Walking this path. Watching, and waiting, and being ready, at any approach, to do enough damage to ensure the bear would never return.

They reached the patch of woods where Elena had shown the creature to Sam. The trail sloped down from the road. The trees were thick. When Elena brought Sam here, the ground was slippery with mud, but the recent heat had dried it. Was that really only two weeks ago? Less? Impossible. It was another lifetime, back when their mother was with them, and Sam was ignorant of her sister's secrets, and none of them could conceive of the ruptures ahead.

"Let's go in," Sam said.

Danny hung back. "I'm pretty sure that's private property."

"Okay?" Sam stepped away from the road, toward the woods, over a log. Branches made a lattice overhead. He wasn't following. As much as it irritated her to admit, she did need him to come along. Did he want to help her sister or what? She told him, "This is where Elena brought me to show me the bear."

He stepped after her. The dog did, too.

The air between the trees moved as gently as a breath. Most of the trunks here were straight and gray, oak and hemlock and fir, but one gangly madrone twisted in front of them. Its bark was peeling already, showing raw orange skin. Berries grew thick on the bushes. The dog sniffed the earth, dropped down, and rolled. Sam couldn't smell the bear's stink. Only the clean summery scent of heated pine, the inland island smell, underlaid with dirt, moss, and salt from the distant shifting tides.

Sam took a seat on a smooth rock. Danny, stopping over her, squinted at the sky. He was less comfortable with her now than he'd been a week earlier. She could see it in his body. He wasn't sure how close they should be.

"You can sit," she said. "If you want. It might be a while."

He paused, considering, then lowered himself to the ground. He was bigger than most of the other men Sam knew. Unwished for, the image of him with Elena, his wide hands and her pale back, flashed before Sam, and she had to shake it out of her mind. Disgusting. What was this thing between them, this not-a-relationship that had stayed in hiding for so long? It didn't make any sense. But it was, Sam supposed, consistent; whatever desperation pushed Elena to try to tame a bear had to be the latest version of the impulse, years earlier, that inspired her to confide in Danny. She'd been frustrated enough to do things entirely inappropriate. Shameful and strange.

At least Danny tried not to be frightening. He made himself into the stuffed toy-store version of a bear or a boyfriend. Shiny-eyed, softly furred. Good for Elena—good choice there—finding someone who could muzzle his viciousness. If only she'd stayed satisfied with that.

"How's work?" he asked.

The dog was exploring the plants around them. Every-thing was dappled from the sunlight through high leaves. "It's fine," Sam said. "Boring."

"But good benefits, right? You get a pension?"

"That's only if you work for the actual ferry system. They didn't hire me. I do concessions instead."

"Ah," he said. "Food and drinks and stuff?"

"Yeah. Exactly." Bittersweet: to think that Elena never talked to him about her. Sam didn't know if it'd feel better to think he knew everything about their family or nothing. It hit as a betrayal from Elena, either way.

"When you got your merchant mariner certification, the idea was that you'd work for the ferry, right?" She nod-ded. "I remember that," he said. "Elena was so excited when she found that course for you."

Oh. So it was worse to think he knew everything. He was talking confidently enough about Sam's past that she was, suddenly, shot through with suspicion: he had some information she didn't. He was going to tell her he'd paid for the certification program. Lent their family money over the years . . . God, she could not stand to have one more secret revealed, she could not take it, enough already. Elena had lied to her, Sam understood, she would forgive. He didn't need to tell her anything else. She said, "Can I hold the gun now?"

He pulled it out. Handed it over.

As soon as she took it from him, her attention sharp-ened. Other thoughts dropped away. There was only the touch of the breeze, the sound of the dog, the vegetal smells that surrounded. Her senses expanded, redirected, and turned toward what she held. What a surprise—its slickness. It felt almost oiled. The pistol was cool weight in her palm.

Such a small thing. Heavy, though. Odd. If she had had this in her hand a month ago . . . the first time the animal came to their door . . . She lifted it, shut one eye, aimed at a high branch.

"The safety's on," Danny said.

"I'm not going to pull the trigger," she said. She was only looking. Remembering. Imagining.

This, in her hand, was at last the feeling Elena had talked about. The deep awareness of her body. The knowledge of all that had been and might be. With this gun, they could've gotten rid of their visitor that very first day. Cracked a living room window, fired a single shot, and seen the bear flee. She and Elena would've gasped and shrieked and clung to each other. They would've gone to the back of the house together and told the whole story to their mom. A bear! So wild! Sitting up in bed, their mother would laugh.

Sam and Elena would repeat the tale to each other over the years. They wouldn't argue about anything. There would be no cause. Madeline would've never gotten in touch, so there would be no charges filed, no fines incurred, no bizarre offers, no consequences. Only a silly, momentary encounter with a feral thing that dashed off as soon as they frightened it—a passing moment in their unbroken sisterhood, which would travel, eventually, from San Juan to some new destination, where they would live in harmony, twin rose trees growing outside.

That was the power a gun carried. It let her believe she could change what was. Danny asked, "All done?"

"Not yet," Sam said. She lowered the gun to her lap. Time passed. The metal, in her grip, warmed, like something alive.

A breeze blew. And then they heard her:

Are you there?

SAM AND DANNY MOVED AGAINST THE BREEZE. THE AIR carried Elena's voice. As they got closer to her, it brought, too, a growing whiff of that meaty stink, the bear's rottenness, its stench. They couldn't see it yet, but it was there. And they were on their way.

The dog moved with them. Its lips were wet. Danny had taken the gun back from Sam, immediately, but not holstered it. He carried it at his side. It radiated power. They were going to take care of this. The bear was not stronger than they were anymore.

Their steps crunched over twigs. Soil compressed underneath. Beside Sam, Danny's breath was quick. In her own ears, her heart was thumping, so loud it might warn the bear they were coming, as loud as a shouted alarm. Her blood was noisy. She stumbled, once, as they went between the trees, but caught herself. She listened as hard as she could through the clamor of her own body for her sister. Closer now. Proximate.

There Elena was. Holding out her arms. Standing before the beast.

Sam and Danny came at them from the side, a bit to the bear's back. Elena was in her uniform with her hair tied up. A normal girl, a pagan priestess. She was offering something, and the animal was massive, rippling, bent over her outstretched hands. It snuffled across them. Danny made a sound at the sight. The bear's enormity. It sat on its haunches. Brown, gold, tipped with white. Its shoulder blades jutted toward the sky.

The dog barked. Elena saw Sam and Danny then. She pulled her hands back, and the bear spun, more agile than Sam would've thought possible, quick and muscular as a monster in a horror movie. The dog's barks shook the air. Sam and Danny were less than a hundred feet away from the bear and Elena; the wind, pushing on their faces, had let them come close without giving signal. The bear stepped away from Elena, paced in place, stepped back.

"What are you doing here?" Elena shouted to them.

Half a loaf of white bread lay on the dirt in front of her. The bear, an arm's length away, was huffing, letting out blasts of hot noise. Danny's dog snapped its teeth and kept on barking. The bear stretched open its mouth. Its jaw popped.

At Sam's side, Danny said, "My god."

Elena said something. To the bear—too quiet for Sam to hear. The bear stepped away again, turned, and faced them. Its front paws danced.

"Back up," Elena shouted their way.

The bear's jaw kept popping. It made a moaning noise.

Over its bottom teeth, a line of saliva spilled out. The dog wouldn't stop barking. They were spooking the bigger animal, Sam could see, and that was good, that was what they'd come to this place to do, they had to teach it to stay away, they had to frighten it that badly. Make it run to the shore it had climbed up off of. Force it back into the sea. Over the dog's barks, Sam said to Danny, "Shoot it." He didn't. She told him again: Shoot it. Now. He wasn't lifting his arm.

"Do it," Sam said, her voice raised to carry over the barking and the slobbering, and she grabbed at Danny's hand. He tried to twist away from her. She got a grip on the gun and pulled. It was cold dense metal under her fingers— it had lost the warmth she'd given. She yanked on it and he tugged away, and though he was bigger, he was less forceful, he didn't want to hurt anyone, she could tell, but she had had enough of his pretending, she knew he was capable of it, and the time had come for hurt. If he wouldn't, she would. She was willing to do what she had to, so she pulled harder, she bore down. All around them was wet sound and popping joints and loud dog and struggle. Elena was yelling. Under Sam's finger, a trigger, a switch. She pressed. It fired.

The bear lunged.

THE MAGIC OF BEING A YOUNGER SISTER: THAT EVERY second of Sam's life, since before she drew her first breath, before she swam inside her mother, and before a stranger's seed ever met the egg that would divide into her growing self, Elena was there. Always. Always Elena. Nothing matched an older sibling's constancy; their mother, Sam knew even before the diagnosis, would die, because parents died before children did, that was the way of the world, and the planet would heat and transform over the years, and pandemics would rip through humanity, but Elena and Sam would keep going, they were permanent. Elena had been beside Sam since before birth and would be there until everything was done. If they fought, if they lied, if Elena told Sam to move out—if Elena yelled insults in a parking lot and Sam ordered their neighbor to fire a bullet—if they went to funerals, or had love affairs, or one got the other in trouble with the sheriff and racked up fines, still, they were sisters, forever, no matter. They were sisters and they would last past the end of time.

Sam knew that. Then the bear. It closed its jaws over Elena's face. Sam saw her sister go.

AFTER, DANNY DIDN'T BLAME SAM. HE BLAMED HIMself. The sheriff's office blamed him, too, for having the gun, agitating the animal; they brought charges for reckless endangerment, but the Larsens got a lawyer, and Danny ended up pleading only to trespassing. From her living room, Sam watched his truck roll up and down their road. No one seemed to stop hiring his company to maintain their lawns. She sometimes heard people mention his name in the grocery store. Sam still had to get groceries, inconceivable as that was to her. She had to eat, in the world where Elena no longer was.

Danny came to their house a single time. Hearing the knock, she knew it had to be him. Who else? They were linked. When she opened the door, she found him, the skin drawn tight over his cheekbones, his forehead creased. His hair was getting shaggy. He said he needed her to know that he loved her sister more than he ever had or ever would love anyone else in the world. He said, "I'm so sorry."

Inside Sam, a swell, a fall. She said, "Me too."

Seeing him made her think again of the way he'd clenched the gun's grip when Sam pulled, required her to return to that day. After that, she hid in the house when he walked his dog. .The animal jumped and smiled. When it barked, Sam flinched. It had known Elena—did it know she was gone? It could blame no one for her absence. It didn't understand the concept of fault.

If Sam's mother were alive, she would've shaken her head at Sam. How could you not trust your sister? she'd have asked. Their mother always insisted Elena knew what she was doing. Sam hadn't believed her enough.

The San Juan *Journal* put the blame on the bear, which, its staff argued in a series of opinion pieces and pointed articles, had for weeks been growing bolder, lessening the distance it kept between itself and humankind. The newspaper said it should've been hauled away by the state ages before. It had broken into someone's empty vacation home near Mount Grant, Sam learned, and ripped the dry goods off their pantry shelves. It turned over barbecues in backyards and raided sheds full of livestock feed.

Madeline Pettit could have publicly blamed Elena for that mounting behavior. Sam knew. Elena's insistence on coming closer to it. The bread she'd held in her cupped hands that very last day. Madeline told them not to bait it, warned them that its actions would escalate in response, but Elena hadn't heeded her, had encouraged it, and the escalation went beyond even what Madeline foretold. Afterward,

Sam waited for the paper to print news of their misde-
meanor. To kill Elena again—this time, her legacy. Why
wouldn't Madeline expose them? Madeline, who had given
so many warnings to their family, and whom time and teeth
had proven right. Instead, Sam received a letter informing
her that, in light of the circumstances, the state was no longer pursuing the matter of Elena's feeding any carnivore.

She got a package, too, from Madeline herself. A neat
cardboard box with a plastic bag of soil inside. It was accompanied by a handwritten note, a single sheet, filled by
meticulous block letters—striking penmanship—but, then,
Sam would expect nothing less. Madeline wrote how very
sorry she was for Sam's loss. What an impression, the few
times they'd met, Elena had made on her. How poised Elena
had seemed. How lovely.

The soil in the box had been collected from the ground
under Elena that day. Growing up, Madeline wrote, she'd
been taught by her mother's family that a person who dies
tragically should be buried with whatever their blood last
touched, and she didn't know whether that belief was
Catholic or Coeur d'Alene, but it was old and had always
rung true to her. It was supposed to give that person peace
in the afterlife. Madeline hoped Sam would forgive her the
liberty.

She didn't write about destroying the bear, though Sam
knew, from her interactions with authorities in the immediate aftermath, that they had. During those first, impossible days, that knowledge was one of the few things Sam was

able to fix on. The state had captured and killed the bear before Elena was cremated. That fast.

And Madeline didn't write about the bear's stomach contents, although Sam understood, from one horrifying late-night search on her phone early on when she could not sleep, that was information forensic biologists sought. Sam knew now about the existence of forensic biologists. She stopped going as much on her phone after that. She wanted to erase from her mind every single thing life had ever taught her, but she wasn't able.

Madeline's note did say that her office learned the bear had been a grizzly after all. Shocking, Madeline called it, and improbable. A grizzly hadn't been seen in their part of Washington in living memory. Madeline wrote that what had happened was a tragedy, and that she very much wished, for both Sam's and Elena's sakes, she could have established the mutual trust that might have allowed for a different outcome.

The note contained no suggestion of the sisters' share, the ways they had blocked Madeline from tracking the animal's movements and habits and shape. But Sam knew. Sam, from the start, had treated Madeline the way her sister ought to have behaved toward the bear. She'd told herself the woman was a danger, and used that as a reason to resist her attraction, and denied, therefore, whatever Madeline offered. Her knowledge. Her state resources. Her availability, her precise kind of care. Sam had shoved all that away while putting her trust in her next-door neighbor and his dumb blond dog, and in her sister, her precious sister, who had been foolish enough to stretch out her arms to a grizzly bear.

Elena . . . As punishment, Sam read Madeline's note dozens of times. Hard evidence of her fatal ignorance.

Sam took more shifts than ever. Their routine helped numb her, though one income wasn't enough to cover the mortgage, obviously. The bank didn't question anyone's role in this disaster. It looked only at the numbers. Late that summer, it initiated the process of taking the house. Sam took down the sheets that Elena had fixed to the living room ceiling and stripped the pillowcases their mother had rested her head on. She counted out Elena's remaining tip money and tucked it away in a suitcase their grandmother left behind.

On the ferry, no one guessed. For a while, snippets of tourists' conversations floated by about animals, accidents, a local girl's misfortune, but none of the passengers would ever suspect that Sam had anything to do with their gossip. To them, she was little more than a servant, wiping their endless crumbs away while they talked of excitement elsewhere. That was fine. She used to get upset when they made her Cinderella. She didn't get upset about that anymore.

Ben found her in the boat's break room. He held her. She let him. Her sister was gone.

He didn't blame her. He sat close beside, he wanted to talk. When she shook, he laid his hand, warm, on her back, and moved it in small circles for long enough that Sam

passed from horror to something like rest. Under their bodies, the floor lifted and sank with the movement of the
waves. Whenever other crew members came in, Ben gestured at them to leave. They understood, he said. He insisted they understand. He told Sam no one could possibly
think it was anyone's fault.

Sam didn't believe that. If she had left with him before,
would that have saved Elena's life? It could've. So might
have a million other shifts—if Elena hadn't gone to work
that day. Or if she had crossed paths with the bear farther
from the spot Sam and Danny chose to sit, so met it, stroked
its face without incident, and moved on. If Elena, instead of
serving at the golf club, had been a waitress at a restaurant
in town, and needed to drive to and from her shifts. That
way, she never, ever would have walked that trail. If she,
instead of Sam, had taken the merchant mariner course ten
years earlier, and gotten hired on the ferry instead. If their
mother hadn't gotten sick. If their mother's boyfriend had
never moved in. If the sisters had, at the very last moment,
gone with Madeline to Mill Creek, and if from that city
they had begun the rest of their traveling lives. Afterward,
Sam spent all her time thinking about these things: who
was responsible, what had brought them here.

How would Elena respond? If she were— That was the
thought Sam couldn't get out of her head. Elena's voice:
You never listen. Or: *I love you.* One, then the other, then
both, then back again. Elena would explain to Sam how
special the bear was, how strange and tender their connec-

tion, and how it would never intentionally hurt her, but if it did, any pain would be worth the intense, extraordinary, world-expanding experience of getting to stand before it and feel its muzzle brush across her palms. She would say it was all right to die, because through the bear, she'd gotten the chance to really live.

Or: Sammy. You saw how much I suffered. You heard the scraping. Bone on bone, fangs on skull. That bear, in the end, showed how pointless every passion we ever held was.

But Elena was gone. Sam would never find out what she thought of what happened. All Sam could hear, now, was her own voice whispering that it was Sam's fault. Wasn't it? No matter what anyone else said or didn't say. Hadn't she known that in the first instant of the bear's lunge and every day after? Sam ate her meals, she went to work, she kept hearing it. She always would. She remembered the trigger guard under her finger. Its curve, its give. Blame became her companion; blame filled the place her sister had occupied.

SAM BOARDED THE FERRY FROM FRIDAY HARBOR, THE seventh sailing leaving the island that fall weekday, for her last trip across San Juan Channel. A deckhand she didn't recognize waved her into position on the car deck. He reminded her to turn off her engine during the ride.

Beyond the deck's open front, water shifted, careless and gray. In the car's trunk, Sam had what was left of Elena, her driver's license and favorite items of clothing, and her cremains mixed with the dirt sent by Madeline.

Some of that mix, Sam had left on the island: on their property, among the trees, in the same spot they'd put their mother's ashes. Unmarked though it was, the place was easy for Sam to find; she and Elena had walked those woods a thousand times. Sam knew the ground and the branches. The camas flowers were past their bloom but the fireweed had come out. She knelt there, as Elena did before, and spread her sister's body. The dirt and ash were cool on her fingers. She pressed until they blended with the ground. The bank might have the deed to the property, but Elena and their mother had become part of the earth. They were under San Juan's lighthouse, the high southern grasses, the bleached white logs on the beaches where Sam and Elena had played as girls.

The rest of the mix, Sam pictured, not for the first time, scattering off the side of this ship, though the channel had borne nothing good toward the sisters, it had carried the bear. But was it a resting place Elena would've wanted? Sam did not, and could not, know. So she kept carrying the dirt and ash along. Other passengers trailed down the narrow aisle between Sam and the neighboring line of vehicles. The water rippled. Once, Sam believed she knew her sister's mind better than anything, but now they were separated from each other.

Elena was gone. Their mother, too. The house. The ideas Sam had held, closer and more valued than stolen jewels, about where the sisters were going—the places they would live, the adventures they would have, the opportunities they would learn to take for granted side by side. Every bit of it was lost.

Her phone buzzed. She lifted it to check: Ben making sure she'd boarded all right. She texted him back to confirm. The phone's background was a picture of them he'd taken one afternoon on a fishing trip. Their heads pressed together, two smiles, the edge of Cascade Lake blurred behind. They had gone there for rainbow trout. When Sam caught one, Ben whooped for her. If another passenger glanced at the screen over her shoulder, they'd never guess what Sam had destroyed. They'd see only sweetness.

The ferry blew its horn. It pulled away from the harbor that had held Sam and Elena's childhood. It would dock at Orcas, Shaw, and Lopez, and then unload itself in Anacortes, where Ben was waiting. He was going to drive with Sam to Oregon. A job, an apartment. His life there, as he described it over again, didn't sound so very different from the one Sam's family had led after all: a working existence, with some debt and some plan.

Sam's eyelids ached. Tender and overtouched. She always had a headache these days. The engine underneath vibrated up through her spine.

The open end of the ferry made an enormous mouth that framed the sea. It moved across the water without mercy, swallowing the fantasies she'd dangled overboard these many years. How many times had Sam taken this trip, watching the boat's spreading wake and dreaming? Waiting, always waiting, for her life to change? And now she had changed it. No matter what she did, her future, empty of Elena, waited ahead.

Sam sat in her shut-off car in the churning bottom of the ferry. Her view was cut in half by the horizon. Clouds above and waves below. A decade of practice had taught her how to pass this ride in imagination, how to spend its sixty-five minutes stretching her heart to a distant shore, so she did that, but not to Anacortes, the mainland where she was going. No, Sam went instead to where she'd come from, what she'd seen. She pulled apart the bloody pieces of her last day with her sister and formed them into something she could take with her. Nearly everything else, she had been forced to leave behind.

She pictured Elena. Elena and the bear. The bear turning to Elena for comfort. It bit into her to be closer, closest, made one. They had died together, Sam told herself; as the boat churned, she collapsed the time between Elena's destruction and the bear's final fall, the time that had distinguished what was being ravaged and what was ravaging. Sam imagined them together. They were wed.

I love it, Elena had told Sam. The bear. She'd said it was nowhere else but their island. She'd said she wanted nothing more. Knowing that, it had embraced her, wrapped its mouth and claws around her, pressed her into San Juan's fragrant ground. The bear freed Elena from her responsibilities, her worries, her pain. The boat's sound was mechanical. Sam let its grinding replace the noises she'd heard rise from her sister that day. In memory, Sam took away any suffering, and gave Elena glory instead.

The intimacy of it. The ecstasy. The bear's body reaching into hers. Elena's last breath rising into the bear's flared nostrils. The bear letting its lips enclose her, the only kiss Sam had ever seen Elena invite.

With all the skill she had of picturing things better than they would ever be, Sam imagined everything better than what had actually been. She imagined Elena as a princess and the bear as an enchanted prince. The bear as a bridegroom and Elena a veiled bride. The two of them as two clasped hands, two cooing doves, the ocean swallowing the offering shore. One held entirely inside the other. Both adoring it. Both transformed.

Sam imagined that Elena was not alone, had not been alone, had in fact died surrounded by the love she'd wanted to be swallowed by. And she told herself Elena knew, in her last moments, that Sam was there, too—that Sam had given her that satisfaction. The sisters were together, then. Exactly as it should have been. After so long moving around each other in a single stale house, missing one another's meaning, trying and failing to make themselves understood, they had, in the end, briefly but beautifully, found each other, the way they once had been united, as children, as babies who stared into each other's round and glossy eyes, as creatures who swam in the same dark chamber of their mother's pulsing womb.

Elena had married the bear and Sam was with her. On San Juan Island. Together. Always. And their mother had witnessed it, somehow, and she wasn't sick, her body had healed miraculously, she grew old in peace beside them, nothing hurt. The world was full of hopes to be realized. Lifelong dreams coming true. Beyond the boat, the water pulled forward toward the rest of Sam's days, but she didn't feel it anymore, she didn't notice, she was only going back to scenic San Juan. She told herself the story of what happened there. In it, the sisters wanted for nothing. They had a kingdom of their own. They were as close as two perfect girls in the fables people offered their children as bedtime stories. Every year, they grew the most beautiful roses, white and red. They lived happily ever after.

ACKNOWLEDGMENTS

THIS BOOK WAS A STRANGE BEAST THAT EMERGED DURING a difficult time. I am forever grateful to Brittany K. Allen, Arif Anwar, Hannah Bae, Andrea Bartz, Jessie Chaffee, Claire Dunnington, Sara Faring, Mira Jacob, Luis Jaramillo, Angie Kim, Crystal Hana Kim, Jean Kwok, Krys Lee, Melissa Rivero, Alizah Salario, Leigh Stein, Boo Trundle, Yoojin Grace Wuertz, and Jung Yun for believing in what it might do.

Suzanne Gluck championed the project from the very start and David Ebershoff led me along the path to bring it into the world. The greatest agent, the greatest editor. I am so lucky to be with the teams at WME and Hogarth, who make the wildest dreams come true.

The book is here thanks to Hedgebrook, the Randolph MFA community, Pen Parentis, #1000wordsofsummer, and the New York Public Library's Center for Research in the Humanities. Its most crucial support came from my family's childcare providers, whose work makes my work happen. All my gratitude goes to Ms. Shevon, Ms. Madeena, Ms. Tiana, Ms. Janice, Ms. Jesse, and Ms. Melissa.

San Juan Island gave me so much. It took from me, too. For both, I am grateful.

Finally, and always, I thank Alex, Max, and Anna. You three are the home I wish for. You are the best of all possible lives. I love you.

ABOUT THE AUTHOR

JULIA PHILLIPS is the bestselling author of the novel *Disappearing Earth,* which was a finalist for the National Book Award and one of *The New York Times Book Review*'s 10 Best Books of the Year. She lives with her family in Brooklyn.

This book was set in Bembo, a typeface based on an old-style Roman face that was used for Cardinal Pietro Bembo's tract *De Aetna* in 1495. Bembo was cut by Francesco Griffo (1450–1518) in the early sixteenth century for Italian Renaissance printer and publisher Aldus Manutius (1449–1515). The Lanston Monotype Company of Philadelphia brought the well-proportioned letterforms of Bembo to the United States in the 1930s.